Murder in the Bluebell Woods

The Wootton Windmill Mysteries
Book 2

Izzie Harper

ASIN for the ebook: B0BRX2MPSQ

ISBN for the paperback: 978-1-7392189-1-1

For Julia Barrett.
RIP.

Chapter 1

DAY 1 - Thursday, 11am

Spring was in mid-flourish in the Kent village of Lower Wootton. It was the day of the wedding and Ellie Blix and her family were in Appledown Woods with their neighbours. In the magnificent canopies of oak, ash and chestnut, the spring songbirds were in full throttle.

The young couple stood in front of Rattling Folly with their celebrant, about to say their vows. Sunlight streamed through tree branches onto the weathered brickwork of the ivy-covered ruins and onto the surrounding carpet of green and purple bluebells.

The groom's sage green waistcoat was a colourful contrast to his black morning suit. He gazed into his bride's eyes. 'I, Adrian Robert Abbott, have chosen to spend my life with you, Jane Mary Lacy. I promise to be loving, loyal and faithful.' He placed a silver band on his bride's finger. 'This ring is a token of my love for you.'

Ellie felt a wistful tug. Her mind drifted to her own marriage. To love, loyalty and fidelity. To Dave, who stood next to her, and from whom she had been separated for eighteen painful months.

High above them in the trees, a woodpecker drummed on dead timber.

The bride, a schoolfriend of Ellie's daughter, wore a floor-length, off-the-shoulder, ivory dress. Her honey-blonde hair had a garland of bluebells woven through it. She reminded Ellie of a flower which had opened in response to the sun.

'I, Jane Mary Lacy have chosen to spend my life with you, Adrian Robert Abbott. I promise to be loving, loyal and faithful.' She placed a ring on the groom's finger and repeated his words.

Ellie had grown up in these woods. She'd grazed her legs climbing the trees, knew all the best hide-and-seek spots, and had fallen off the rope swing in the dug-out more times than she could remember.

Even had her first kiss here at the folly with Dave.

'Doesn't she look beautiful?' she whispered to him.

He nodded, gently putting his finger to his lips. A tender smile crossed his face and Ellie wondered how the vows made him feel. He lowered his arm, and, for a few electric moments, his fingers flickered next to Ellie's.

'You may kiss your bride,' the celebrant announced.

Adrian cradled Jane's chin in the palms of his hands. He paused for a few moments while he took in his wife, and then, very slowly, he leant in and gave her a gentle kiss.

Cheers and whoops erupted in the woodland. People began moving about, greeting friends and commenting on the ceremony. Some made their way over to the 'wishing tree', to read the notes which hung from branches with a small, silver bell on pieces of purple and green ribbon.

Prosecco corks popped in quick succession.

'What's the plan then?' Dave asked his family.

'Adding our notes to the wishing tree,' Zoe replied to her dad. She gestured to the giant oak which was a fluttering of purple and green, and a tinkling of bells. 'Drinks here in the wood, then back to the village hall for food and dancing.' She looked her dad up and down approvingly. 'Check *you* out, Mr Charcoal Suit.'

Ellie slid her arm round her twenty-two-year-old daughter's waist.

'Except,' said Ellie's mother-in-law, Sylvia, sternly, '*some of us* have got cleaning to do and cakes to bake. The open day is in three days.'

Ellie's phone vibrated in her jacket pocket.

'Chill, Gran,' Zoe chipped in. 'We'll all help. Let's have fun today.' She linked her arm with her father's. 'You'll help too, won't you, Dad? Be at the windmill on open day?'

Ellie and Dave rolled their eyes at each other. Their daughter had spent the past four months trying to get them back together.

'That's up to your mother,' Dave said affectionately.

'She wants you to come too. Don't you, Mum?' Zoe adopted her well-perfected pleading look.

'Let's see how things pan out.' Ellie trailed her hand over Zoe's long, curly hair. 'Your dad might be working.' She changed the subject. 'Shall we have a drink? Toast the couple?' She got out her phone to check who was ringing.

Two missed calls from one of her cleaning company customers.

'I'll have a soft drink,' said Dave, who was a detective inspector in the local police. 'It's my day off but the team are two officers down. If anything happens, it's likely I'll be called in.'

Zoe's boyfriend, Finn, who was also in his twenties, peeled away and headed over towards the trestle table where glasses and Prosecco awaited the guests. He stopped and chatted briefly with two old schoolfriends from the village. All three looked smart in tailored waistcoats over crisp, white shirts.

Ellie dialled into her voicemail.

'Hello Ellie, dear. Gladys Blackman calling to let you know that I've cancelled my contract with Blix Blitz and...'

Ellie's heart sank as she rang off. Not another cancellation. She had only just got the business stable again. The last thing she wanted was a return to the exhaustion of a few months earlier. She'd give Gladys a call. Find out what was going on.

Finn returned with four glasses of Prosecco and a bottle of water for Dave. He handed out the drinks.

But Ellie couldn't get Gladys' call off her mind. 'I think I'll nip back to the windmill and get Rebus. Anyone fancy a quick walk with the dog?'

'I'll come,' Zoe said. 'I saw a woodpecker yesterday down by the stream and want to check if he's still there.'

One of the things Ellie liked about Wootton was that the village clustered around the green and, from her home at the windmill, she could get to most places within twenty minutes, including the seafront. Appledown Woods and the high street were a five-minute walk.

Ten minutes later, Ellie had collected Rebus, the cockerpoo, and she and Zoe were back in the woods, making their way along the flinty path.

After a bitter winter, spring was like a warm blanket. In the dappled sunshine, Ellie – who had ditched her kitten-heeled slingbacks for chunky trainers – followed along behind Zoe, smiling at her daughter's pairing of knee-length, black wellies with the flared midi dress from the wedding.

Ellie stopped and crouched amongst the bluebells, admiring the delicate purple trumpets, and drinking in their strong, sweet scent.

Zoe was studying a nest high up in the trees. 'Any news on the burglary?'

A house – belonging to the village butcher – had been broken into a couple of days earlier.

'Not that I've heard. Hopefully, it was a one-off.'

'Everyone's excited about the open day. Finn's been checking the RSVPs and Dad reckons we're going to need extra parking.'

'I'm glad they're taking care of that then,' Ellie replied. 'The spring one always raises the most money. When I send the donations, the Stroke Association can never believe the amount.'

'I reckon we're going to smash it this year,' Zoe said. 'We've got lambs, bluebells... *and* the windmill.'

The striking landmark had been in Ellie's family for generations, back to the days when it was used for milling wheat.

'And our secret weapon is Gran's lush cakes.'

Ellie got up and followed Zoe along the path towards the stream. Rebus darted back and forth through the undergrowth, sniffing out smells and following trails. At this time of year, the woods were teeming with mice, shrews and voles.

'The woodpecker was here somewhere,' said Zoe. 'Yes, there.' She pointed to a silver birch. 'Listen.'

The bird drummed at the wood.

Rebus shot past and plunged into the stream. He sloshed about, tail wagging, submerging his nose.

'I'm sure that dog is half otter,' Ellie said with a chuckle. 'Ever since he was a puppy, he's loved water. Seems to enjoy the cool feeling on his paws.'

Rebus started digging excitedly at the bed of the stream, like he'd found buried treasure. After a moment or two, he produced a filthy stick. He was enjoying himself so much it was hard not to watch him and wonder what was going on in his head.

Ellie was walking towards the birch. The sun was streaming through the branches onto its beautiful white bark. She was about to tell Zoe about Gladys Blackman cancelling her cleaning contract when something caught her attention over by the holly bush, like somebody had dumped a load of old clothes.

'Look at that. What sort of person leaves rubbish this far into the woods?' She strode towards the pile, outraged by the desecration of this beautiful place. But as she approached, she felt herself slowing down. Hairs prickled on the back of her neck.

An outstretched hand.

Fingers.

The worn soles of a pair of shoes, attached to trousered legs.

It was a body. Lying face down. With an arrow in the middle of its back.

'What on earth?' Ellie's legs went weak.

A rush of nausea.

Pulse racing, she spun round, not wanting Zoe to see it.

But Zoe was still sloshing about in the stream in her wellies with the dog.

Ellie turned back and inched closer, her mind churning.

The body was still.

Was the person dead?

Come on. *Think, think.*

What should she do?

Should she check for a pulse or just call 999?

'Zoe, love,' Ellie called, trying to keep her voice calm. 'Put Rebus on the lead, could you? And stay where you are.'

'What's happened?' Distracted and ignoring Ellie's instruction, Zoe jumped out of the stream.

'No, stay there. Someone's been hurt. We need to call Dave and make sure that none of the wedding party come over here.'

'Who is it? Can you see?' Zoe must have spotted the arrow in the person's back.

'No, not from here, and I don't want to get any closer because the police will need to examine the scene.'

'Rebus, come, boy.' Zoe clipped the lead onto the dog's collar. 'Hold on. I recognise that hoodie. It's got the farm shop logo on the back. It must be Robert Seale. He was the only person who wore it.'

'Are you certain?'

'Yeah, Mum. He came up to the wood yard wearing it. I recognise his hair too.'

Ellie pulled her phone from her coat pocket and tapped the screen. She dialled Dave's number. His voicemail clicked in, so she left a message and rang Sylvia, who answered promptly.

Ellie told her about Robert's body. 'Is Dave still with you?'

'No, he's had to leave.' Sylvia's tone was sombre. 'Is Robert definitely dead?' As an ex-social worker who had been married to a detective, Sylvia was ever the pragmatist.

'Pretty sure.'

Ellie knew Robert a bit through his wife, Tracy. Like Ellie, Tracy had lived in the village all her life, and they'd attended the same schools.

Zoe joined Ellie and positioned the phone so she could hear the conversation.

'I'll ring 999 as soon as we hang up,' Ellie told Sylvia. 'Is Tracy still in the clearing with the kids?'

'Yes.'

In her mind, Ellie kept seeing Robert's body. She was struggling to focus, to think what was needed. 'Can you ask Finn to stay with Tracy? Keep her there. It would be awful if she and the children went wandering and found him. Don't mention that anything has happened to Robert.'

'Righto.'

'What about Liam? Is he still there too?'

Liam was Tracy's eldest son, one of the friends that Finn had chatted to when he'd got their drinks.

'Hang on. I'll have a look.' The line went silent for a few moments. 'No sign of him.'

'OK. It's probably a good idea to speak to the bride and groom too. Let them know there's been a serious incident and the police will be coming.'

'Will do.'

'I'll stay here with the body until the police arrive. Just in case any of the families go off-piste or walkers come by.' Ellie rang off.

'Shall I take Reeby home and go back to the clearing?' Zoe suggested. 'Help Gran and Finn to keep everyone there?'

'That's a good idea.'

'Who's done this, Mum?' Zoe's eyes were wide with alarm.

Ellie felt a protective pang and put her arm round her daughter. She was wondering the same thing. By the looks of it, the person responsible was a skilled archer. Lots of the locals did archery. But, as far as she knew, they didn't shoot people in the woods.

Who on earth did?

This wasn't the Wild West. It was a bluebell wood in a tiny village on the south coast of England. The largest creatures they saw here were rabbits, squirrels and foxes. Very occasionally a deer.

'There was a mouse on Robert's legs just a moment ago,' said Zoe. 'The wildlife have got used to the body being on the ground.'

'That's a good point.'

'And Finn and Adrian were here last night around 9pm, checking that everything was OK for the wedding,' Zoe told her mum. 'Robert's body can't have been here then or they would've seen it.'

'That will narrow down the time of death even further.' As Ellie spoke, an important detail dawned on her. If someone had entered the woods carrying a bow and arrow, there was a high chance they would have been seen. Surely?

Chapter 2

12pm

In the clearing, the wedding guests were milling about, chatting, laughing and sipping drinks.

Sylvia was kicking herself for letting Zoe talk her into wearing a maxi dress with three-quarter length sleeves. Right now, she wished she was wearing her comfy jeans and fleece. 'The police will be here any minute,' she told Finn. She had taken him to one side and told him about the body by the stream.

Poor chap was ashen.

Sylvia put her arm round his shoulders. He wasn't much older than Zoe, didn't have any siblings, and his mother had died four months earlier. This was bound to dredge up painful memories for him. 'Tracy's over by the folly with the kids and her sister,' she said softly. 'Do you want to have a word with them? See if you can persuade them to stay here until the police arrive?'

'OK, Sarge.' Finn put his hand to his head in a mock-salute and scuttled off.

Sylvia smiled. Finn wasn't being disrespectful, and she appreciated that Zoe's boyfriend felt able to be cheeky with her. He wasn't her grandson, but over the last few months he'd started to feel like it. Since her husband's death, it was closer family contact that was making Sylvia want to sell her house in Deal and move back to Wootton permanently.

She spotted the bride and groom by the drinks table, talking to the celebrant. For a moment, she thought of the flicker of hope that she'd seen in Ellie's eyes earlier when she'd looked at Dave. She was sure she wasn't imagining it. Was their time coming back round? She hoped so.

Sylvia pulled the ridiculous pins out of her hair, wrapped her scarf round her shoulders and made her way over to speak to the couple. It was their day, so they would be best placed to ask everyone to stay put. 'I'm afraid I have bad news,' she told them. 'I'm deliberately keeping my voice low so that only you four can hear me. There has been, I don't know what to call it, an *incident* over by the stream.'

'An incident? Sylvia you're sounding very *official*.' Adrian chortled, as though he thought a wedding prank was in the offing.

'I'm afraid I'm not joking. I wish I was.' She paused and waited until she had their attention so that she didn't have to raise her voice. 'Someone has been seriously hurt and Ellie has called the police.' She let the news sink in. 'My late husband was in the force. They will want everyone to remain here so they can talk to us all. Ellie is going to stay where she is until the police arrive.'

'What's happened?' Jane looked at her new husband hopefully, as though he would know what to do. 'Who is it? This is awful.'

Adrian clutched his floppy hair. 'It was an accident, right?'

Chapter 3

12pm

'Hang on,' Zoe said. 'What's that?'

Ellie turned to see what she was talking about. They were waiting for the police to arrive.

'There's someone's phone. Look.' Zoe crept closer to the body to see properly.

A mobile phone was lying face down on the leaves and mud next to Robert. On the cover, a woman had her arms round two children and was smiling at them.

Ellie's thoughts were spinning. 'It's Tracy's. How did it get here?''

ele

Around twenty minutes later, the police arrived, accompanied by scene-of-crime vehicles, an ambulance and various unmarked cars. Within moments, the incident scene was taped off.

Dave approached Ellie, his face grim. He was still wearing his charcoal wedding suit. 'Can you tell me what you saw when you got here?'

She filled him in. They'd found the body while they were walking the dog. Then recognised the hoodie and saw Tracy's mobile phone.

'Are Zoe and Mum back at Rattling Folly?'

'Yes. Zoe's taken Rebus home and then she's going to join Sylvia and Finn.'

'That's OK. My sergeant will be there to sort everything out.' He looked like he was about to walk away when he stopped and said in a low voice, 'Ellie, I'm really pleased you and I are back on good terms, but when Andrea was killed, it was really difficult with you, Mum and Zoe sleuthing about...' He cleared his throat. 'So, at the risk of sounding like a complete jerk...'

She knew what was coming.

'... could I please request that you stay out of this one?'

'Oh... gosh... er...' She stammered. She turned away from him. 'Andrea's death was different. I knew her. Robert Scalc is nothing to do with me.' She shrugged. 'Anyway – I've got enough on my plate with customers cancelling their cleaning contracts.'

Dave sighed with relief before showing concern. 'Sorry to hear about the business. OK to chat about that another time?'

Ellie nodded.

'Thanks for guarding the body. The team will clear the woods and find out if anyone saw anything. Was Tracy at the wedding with the kids? I didn't see her.'

'Yes, she was there and the younger children were with her. Liam was with Charlie Matthews.'

'Does anyone else apart from you, Finn, Mum and Zoe know who the victim is?'

'Not as far as I know.'

Dave nodded.

'I mean, no one else was here with us,' Ellie continued. 'But I have no idea whether anyone else saw the body before we got here.'

Chapter 4

2.15pm

'I'm their main suspect.' Tears were streaming down Tracy's cheeks as she stood on the doorstep of the windmill. 'If I go to prison, what's going to happen to the children?'

Ellie felt a surge of concern for the woman she'd known all her life. She placed her notepad on the table by the door and shifted her attention from her cleaning business to Tracy.

The spring sunlight slanted in through the open door, falling on Tracy's conker-brown hair.

Ellie shuffled backwards, holding Rebus' collar, so Tracy could come in.

'Thanks for having Kieran and Emily,' Tracy said. 'I hope they've been OK.' She eased her shoes off and left them by the door.

The windmill, which had been in Ellie's family for several generations, was open plan downstairs and had a spiral staircase running up the middle of the building.

Ellie led Tracy round the stairs to the lounge and gestured to a sofa. 'They've been as good as gold. Zoe and Finn have been looking after them. They all took Rebus over to the duck pond earlier, and Zoe gave them some toast. They're playing a game upstairs.'

'Thank you. I couldn't call or text. The police have kept my phone for evidence.'

Dave hadn't told Ellie anything about their investigation and she hadn't asked. He was very strict about police confidentiality and had been furious with Ellie a few months earlier when she had listened to one of his conversations and acted on it.

'Are they treating it as a suspicious death then?' She felt protective towards Tracy, who was younger than her.

'Think so. There was no mention of it being an accident. Thing is, I haven't been anywhere near the woods. I've no idea how my phone got there.' Her eyes flashed with shock and anger.

'They look at people known to the victim first of all,' Sylvia said.

'Well, that's me. They've made it pretty clear I'm their number-one suspect.' Tracy sniffed and dabbed at her cheeks with a tissue. 'The kids can't lose me *and* their dad.' She faced Ellie, cheeks tinged red. 'You three did such an amazing job before Christmas, discovering who killed Andrea. Could you... Would you make a few inquiries and find out what happened? If it comes to it – help me clear my name?'

'Oh, Tracy, I can't,' Ellie replied. 'I'm so sorry. It caused such a lot of problems with Dave last time. And he literally asked me in the woods just now not to get involved.'

Tracy nodded sadly.

Threads of guilt tugged at Ellie. She didn't know Tracy as well as her sister, Sally, who was Ellie's best friend. But they'd all gone to the same school, and Tracy had always been around when Ellie played and stayed at their house. Then, as adults, she and Tracy had been on the school's Parent Teacher Association. They'd also worked on a campaign recently against a greedy property developer. The man had cornered Ellie in the cloak room after a planning meeting and Tracy had arrived just in the nick of time.

Sylvia appeared, carrying a tray which she placed on the coffee table. On it were three steaming mugs and a plate of meringues dipped in chocolate. 'If you can prove you weren't in the woods, they'll find out how your phone got there,' Sylvia said. 'Sugar and milk there, if you have it,' she told Tracy.

'Is it just the phone's location that's bothering you?' Ellie asked. 'Or is there something incriminating on it that you're worried about the police seeing?'

'Both. But they'll find lots of angry texts between Robert and me.' Tracy's jaw clenched.

Ellie sat back down.

'We haven't been getting on for a long time. And his temper has been much worse over the last few years.'

'Sorry to hear that.' Ellie knew Robert's temporary role as manager of the local farm shop hadn't gone well, but she didn't know the details.

Upstairs, Ellie heard a door open and a couple of moments later Zoe appeared down the spiral staircase. She was nervously playing with her hair.

'Mum, I'm afraid I've got bad news.'

'What is it?' Ellie asked.

Zoe gestured to the floor above. 'The door's shut. Kieran and Emily can't hear us.'

'Good.'

'Katie Douglas from the *Wootton Gazette* has just posted an article online in the local newspaper.'

'Oh no.' Dread glugged in Ellie's stomach. She had known Katie for several years. The woman was ruthless.

Zoe shifted her glance to Tracy. 'I'm really sorry but the article is about your husband. Somehow, she's got hold of all of the information and it's there for everyone to read.'

'Has she named him?' Tracy's voice was a whisper.

'I'm afraid so.'

'Where on earth would she have got the information from? The police haven't released it yet and they've asked everyone not to divulge it.'

Ellie stood up. She walked to Zoe and gave her a hug. 'Thanks for letting us know. That woman is a piece of work. She has been a journalist for years. She's no rookie. She will know that she's not supposed to publish that information until the police say so. More importantly, though, I wonder who her source was.'

'Here you go, Mum. It's on my phone. It mentions you too. It's not very... complimentary, unfortunately.'

'Let me see.'

Zoe held her phone out for Ellie to look at and swiped the screen.

'Read it out, Ellie, can you?' Sylvia asked.

Ellie cleared her throat. 'Here we go. *Lower Wootton Exclusive. Disgraced local man, Robert Seale, was found dead in Appledown Woods earlier this morning, with an arrow in his back. The body was found by local cleaner and part-time amateur sleuth, Ellie Blix, who the paper last had dealings with when she was investigating the death of Andrea Burdett, who had had an affair with her husband.'*

Ellie stopped reading. 'You wait till I get my hands on Katie. What a complete and utter cow.' She carried on.

'*We can exclusively report an intriguing aspect of this tragic murder. Is it a coincidence that Mr Seale was shot with a bow and arrow when archery equipment was stolen from a local property recently?*'

'How on earth does Katie know that I found the body?' Ellie asked. 'And how does she know that he had an arrow in his back and that Tracy's phone was there?'

'There are only three ways Katie could have got hold of that information.' Sylvia was in strident mode. 'Number one, she has a police contact who has leaked the information to her. That wouldn't surprise me. Last year, she told you that the editor of the paper, Harry, has – or had – a contact in one of the labs who leaked test results to him.'

'That's right. I remember.'

'Number two, someone found that body before you and Zoe did and that person has given her the information. And, number three—'

'... the person who killed Robert has given Katie the information.' Ellie couldn't stop herself from interrupting.

Through the windmill window, Ellie saw Liam, Tracy's grown-up son, parking the car, here to collect his mum and stepsiblings. 'Here's your lift. Do you want to get the kids, Zoe, love?'

Sylvia asked, 'Before you go: have either you or your ex-husband done any archery training?'

Tracy's eyebrows shot up into her hair. 'Andy has, yes. Quite the shot, I believe, too.'

Chapter 5

3pm

Ten minutes later, Tracy and the children had gone home and Ellie, Sylvia, Zoe and Finn were sitting around the kitchen table in the windmill, discussing Tracy's request for the Blixes to investigate Robert's murder.

'I feel bad, saying no to Tracy,' Ellie said. 'She's in trouble and I owe her.' She tore open a family size bag of Doritos and put them in the middle of the table. 'When I was at that planning meeting, if she hadn't arrived when she did, I've no idea what that property developer might have done.' The memory was still vivid.

Fetching her coat.

The musty cloakroom.

Half-drawn curtains.

Turning round and finding the man standing over her.

'It wouldn't hurt to ask a few discreet questions,' said Sylvia, her eyes gleaming with excitement. 'It was such fun last time.'

Ellie enveloped Sylvia in a hug. She adored her mother-in-law's spirit but found her a bit over-enthusiastic sometimes. 'It really annoyed Dave though – and in the woods earlier, he specifically asked me not to.'

'We don't have to do anything that steps on the toes of the police,' Sylvia wasn't going to give up. 'It would complement their work.'

'Actually, that's true,' said Zoe. 'With Finn's mum's murder, we found out stuff that the police didn't.' She looked at her boyfriend. 'Tell her, Finn.'

Finn shook his head. 'I'll forever be grateful to you for finding out who killed Mum, and I'm happy to help out on this one if you decide to take it on, but the decision's not mine.'

'I know we did, but the problem is, Zoe, we are all like dogs with bones once we get going. I did so many things last time which...' Ellie stopped. 'It can't be easy for your dad, having the three of us running round, asking questions.'

'S'pose,' Zoe said.

'And I do need to focus on Blix Blitz – otherwise I'm going to have to lay off the staff I took on and go back to cleaning full-time.' Ellie closed her eyes as she said it, dreading the thought of that happening.

'That's true,' Zoe added. 'You've only just got Blix Blitz back on its feet. Now we've got customers cancelling their cleaning contracts. Plus, it's taken a year for you and Dad to start talking again.'

'Zoe's right,' Sylvia piped up. 'Ignore me. I just want to investigate because I find it interesting.' She gave Ellie an apologetic smile. 'You know, ever since you were a kid, you've never been able to rest when people you care about are in trouble.'

'It's true, Mum.' Zoe looked at her boyfriend. 'You were like that with Finn.'

'At school, whenever someone needed help, you were always one of the first people to offer,' Sylvia continued. 'Do you remember that time when Sally and Andrea were excluded from school? It was one of the first things Dave told me about you. He said you'd marched into the head's office and announced that it wasn't fair, and Dave asked afterwards if you could come for tea.'

Zoe beamed at her mum. 'I didn't know about that. That's so cool.' She paused, as though she was thinking about the implications.

'I hadn't really thought about it like that.' Ellie gave an embarrassed smile.

'But you need to look after yourself, Mum, too. You've got a lot on at the moment.' Zoe took a couple of Doritos and put one in her mouth.

As they were talking, a news bulletin came on the TV in the lounge.

'*Kent Police have launched a murder investigation after a man was found dead in Appledown Woods earlier today.*'

'Turn it up,' said Sylvia.

They all dashed over to the TV and gathered round.

'*Detectives have not yet released the name of the man and are appealing for anyone with any information about what happened to come forward.*'

Finn gasped. 'That's just reminded me of something.'

They all stared at him.

'I don't suppose you took a photograph of the arrow that Robert was shot with, did you?'

'No, I didn't. I must admit I considered it, but I knew Dave would be furious. I had a good look at it though. Slim and shiny. Light grey, and it had small feathers on the end. I'll tell you exactly what it reminded me of. One of Dave's darts except obviously much longer. The set that Zoe gave him for Christmas.'

'I know the ones you mean,' Finn said. 'They're carbon. Charlie had a few at my place a while back.'

'The police don't seem to know who was responsible for the burglary, do they?' Sylvia asked. 'There hasn't been an arrest.'

'No. Mention it to Dave, Finn, just in case,' Ellie said. 'I mean, theoretically the information should be on the police database but I'm not sure if details from burglaries are always shared with murder investigations.'

A heavy feeling crept over Ellie and she felt scared for Tracy and her three children. If Tracy could prove she wasn't in the woods, the discovery of her phone shouldn't incriminate her, but it wouldn't help that she and Robert were on bad terms.

Something else was bothering her though. Why had Tracy been so quick to say that Andy was a good archer?

Chapter 6

4pm

E llie and Sylvia were in the local pub, the Windmill Inn. The sixteenth century building was one of Ellie's many 'second homes' in the village, simply because it was next door to her house.

The place was bustling.

It was that strange time of year when it was still cold enough to light open fires even though they weren't really essential. The two of them were sitting in front of one with Rebus, who was stretched out on the hearth, lapping up the heat.

Sylvia was sipping a large glass of white wine and Ellie had a gin and tonic. On the table between them was Ellie's notepad and pen and a packet of cheese and onion crisps which they were sharing.

'Did Gladys give a reason for cancelling?' Sylvia said. 'Poor lady. At her age, she probably found it confusing.'

'From what I gather, another company approached her,' Ellie said. 'They're cheaper. But she didn't realise they aren't Blix Blitz, so she's going to get her daughter to speak to them.'

'Is this other company pretending to *be* Blix Blitz then?' Sylvia stuffed a crisp into her mouth.

'Think so. Gladys has chucked out the leaflet she had through the door so I'm not certain what they're saying. I've posted on my Facebook page, asking for anyone who's had a leaflet to contact me.'

'Well done.'

'And Zoe's posted an anonymous ad in the Lower Wootton Facebook group, saying she's looking for a cleaner. Hopefully this other company will respond.'

A waitress trundled past with two steaming plates of food.

'I think we're going to need another packet of crisps, don't you?' said Sylvia. 'You seem to have eaten most of these.'

Ellie widened her eyes in mock surprise. 'Actually, I've managed to eat about *three* so far. But you go ahead. I'm eating later. I've got a picnic date.'

Sylvia almost knocked over her wine glass. 'Who with?'

'I know you are the epitome of diplomacy...' She threw Sylvia a cheeky look, '... but I can't tell you that, I'm afraid. We want to keep it low-key.'

Eighteen months ago, Dave had begun a brief affair with a woman in the village. Ellie had been devastated when she found out, not least because the woman was someone she had once been best friends with.

'*We?*' Sylvia said. 'Does Dave know about this?'

'Yes, I've told him.'

'Who else knows?'

'Only Zoe. She heard me arranging it.'

'How do you feel? Are you excited?'

Ellie patted her chest. 'Yes, and mildly terrified. But it's time to get back on the horse. Or give its neck a stroke at least.'

Sylvia looked like she was gathering her words. 'Look, I know I'm just the ex-mother-in-law, but I'm thrilled about this.' She beamed at Ellie and gave her a knowing look. 'Seriously, I might come across as a nosy old bag sometimes, but I'm chuffed to bits.'

'*Sometimes?*'

Sylvia snatched up the crisps.

'*Joking.* You never come across as nosy. I don't know what I would have done without you coming to stay before

Christmas – and, as ex-mothers-in-law go, you are the best.'

Sylvia sniffed and pretended to dab at her nose with a tissue.

'So far, that is.' Ellie sat back to avoid the playful slap she knew would come her way.

'Hello, you two. Sorry to interrupt.' It was Sally, Ellie's best friend. 'Do you mind if I join you? I wanted to talk to you about a couple of things.' Sally's usually cheerful face was clouded with worry.

'Go for it,' Ellie said. 'Grab a drink and pull up a chair. Where's Pete?'

'Actually, that's what I wanted to talk to you about.' She pulled off her coat and hung it on the back of a nearby chair, then tucked her leg underneath her and sat down opposite Ellie and Sylvia. 'Something strange is going on with Pete, I'm sure of it.'

'Do you want something to drink?' Sylvia asked, getting up. 'I'll get you one. You talk to Ellie.'

'White wine please. Thank you.'

Sylvia headed for the bar.

'I do love Sylvia,' Sally said.

'You can have her. She wants to move to Wootton. Permanently.' Ellie pulled a mock-horrified face. 'Just kidding. We love her. Even though she *still* hasn't stopped moving things around in my kitchen.' She recalibrated. 'Come on, then. Tell me what's been going on.'

'So... a couple of nights ago, Pete and Tracy's husband, Robert, were doing a lot of texting. Pete and I were watching a film. That's how I know who he was texting because his phone kept pinging and I asked him who he was getting messages from.'

'Is it unusual, then, for the two of them to text each other?'

'*Very*. They're not friends at all. That's why it made me wonder what was going on. He said they were from Robert and it was about work, which confused me a bit because they don't have business connections anymore.'

'Right.'

'So, I asked Pete if it was more aggro and he didn't say no. He simply said, "Don't worry, it's nothing I can't handle".'

'And he didn't elaborate?'

Sally shook her head. 'I let it go at that point because we were in the middle of watching the film and I just thought I'd pick up the conversation with him again later. But I forgot. Until this morning. I went round to Tracy's first thing to borrow some shoes for the wedding. Luna had chewed the ones I was going to wear. When I got back home, Pete had only just got in from work. Well, that's where he said he'd been. And he was bundling a load of clothes into the washing machine.'

'Doesn't he normally do his own washing?'

'He does. It was the *way* he was doing it. There was something sort of urgent about it. Plus Pete is fanatical about saving money on bills and not causing unnecessary damage to the environment.'

'He's a keeper.'

'He always sorts the washing into whites and coloureds. It's not something that all blokes do, but Pete does. I've always found it really sweet. But what was weird was that he was ramming a white T-shirt into the machine with a dark sweatshirt and a pair of jeans. All together. And they had what looked like blood on them.'

'Blood? Jeez, Sal. Did you ask him what he'd been doing?'

'I was about to, but a delivery van arrived and there was mayhem. You know how narrow the road is outside our place. I was trying to get ready for the wedding and there wasn't much time. I just assumed he must have spilled something on them and wanted to get the stain out quickly. Maybe cut his finger with a pruning knife or something like that.'

'Could he simply have been taking swift action? I know from doing clients' laundry, you have to wash blood quickly. And the first rinse needs to be in cold water.'

'I guess it's possible. Then we dashed off to the wedding and as soon as it finished, Pete disappeared again, and I haven't seen him since. So, I still haven't had the chance to ask him about the texting or the washing.'

'*Or the blood*,' said Ellie emphatically.

'I've rung him but he's not answering.'

'Hmm.'

'There was something else though,' Sally continued. 'It wasn't just his clothes that were muddy. His boots were too. I must've registered that something was unusual about this. He doesn't normally come back from the garden centre with muddy clothes or boots. I mean, obviously they're planting things in the beds, but the soil they use usually has quite a lot of compost and sand in it. It's not chalky mud.'

'That is strange.' Ellie saw deep concern in her friend's eyes.

'The mud made me think of the woods. When he walks Luna, his boots are often like that, covered in mud and leaves.'

'What sort of leaves were these?' Ellie asked.

'Triangular shape. Rounded bottom where the stalk is, with serrated edges?'

'Silver birch,' Ellie said. 'Loads of them by the stream and around the folly.'

Sally threw her hands open. 'I'm worried that he's involved with something dodgy. I can't tell the police in case it incriminates him.'

'Sal...'

Earlier, Ellie had been worried about Tracy coming under suspicion. Now, there was definitely something off in what Sally was saying about Pete. But he was a decent man. There was bound to be a simple explanation, surely?

The conversation moved on and Sylvia returned with a glass of wine for Sally and another round of drinks for Ellie and her.

'Thanks, Sylvia. Bless you.' Sally pointed at the fresh glass of wine that Sylvia had just placed next to her own finished one. 'Are you two celebrating?'

'*Yes,*' Sylvia pronounced at the same time as Ellie said, '*No.*'

The three of them laughed in unison.

'Ellie's got a *date* this evening,' Sylvia whispered across the table. 'A picnic.' She tapped the side of her nose and winked.

'Why didn't I know about this? I'm your best friend.'

'Oh God. I knew this was going to happen.' Ellie covered her face with her hands.

'She didn't tell *anyone*,' Sylvia whispered and did an exaggerated scan of their surroundings. 'They wanted to keep it top secret.'

'You should take up amateur dramatics,' Ellie told Sylvia.

'What about Dave?' Sally asked.

'Time for a fresh start,' Ellie replied.

'Well. I hope you have a thoroughly gorgeous evening, and I can't wait to hear all about it.' Sally put out her hand and touched Ellie's arm. 'Changing the subject – how is my sister? I've not seen her since the wedding as the police were with her.'

Tracy was six years younger than Sally.

'Understandably distraught,' Ellie answered. 'The police have her as their main suspect at the moment. She asked us to investigate.'

Sally let out a sigh of relief. 'I'm so pleased you're going to. I was going to ask but—'

'I'm sorry, Sal. I can't. I told her no.'

'Are you sure?'

Ellie explained the reasons. 'We discussed it last night and agreed we wouldn't.'

'Would you reconsider?'

Ellie and Sylvia glanced at each other.

'I'm worried that Pete might be involved, so you'd be doing *me* a favour as well as Tracy.'

Ellie was chewing the side of her cheek. When she said no to Tracy she didn't know about Pete's behaviour. 'Well... I'm not promising anything, but I'll *think* about it.'

Sally put her hands together in a prayer gesture. 'Thank you. Tracy needs a break. She and Robert haven't got on well for ages.'

'She mentioned that.'

Sally was nodding. 'It's true, unfortunately. I've been begging her to leave him for a few years now.'

'Ladies.' A familiar voice interrupted them from behind.

They all turned.

It was Dave, holding a picnic hamper, beaming at Ellie. 'Are you ready?'

A blush crept into her cheeks.

'He's your—' Sylvia said, far too loudly.

'I'm not very good at picnics but you can't go wrong with Waitrose deli, can you? Olive, anyone?'

Chapter 7

5pm

'Mum's face was priceless,' Dave said to Ellie as they crossed Pennypot Lane and walked onto the village green.

'I know.' She chuckled. 'I feel a bit mean.'

'I take it you didn't say you were going out with me?'

'Couldn't resist teasing them.'

'Where would you like to go? We could sit by the duck pond or—'

'How about the folly?' said Ellie. 'It's more private and so pretty there with the bluebells.'

'I'm up for that. The crime scene's been released and it's quite a way from Rattling Folly anyway.'

'How's the case going?'

'Early days. And you know I can't tell you anything.'

They passed the duck pond. A gaggle of ducks was gliding through the water, quacking boisterously.

'Zoe said she saw the chicks earlier.' Dave put his phone on silent and stuffed it in his pocket. 'I was beginning to wonder if you were ever going to agree to come out with me,' he said, his features softening into a gentle smile. 'I wasn't going to give up, you know.'

This was news to Ellie. 'I'm glad you didn't.' While she had continued to say no, she'd worried he'd get impatient with her. He hadn't, and it made Ellie love him that little bit more.

He touched her arm softly and guided her towards the path beside the church. It was a small, simple gesture but Ellie felt a surge of longing.

The path was just wide enough for them to walk side by side, but it meant walking closer together and Ellie felt Dave's body warm hers.

As they moved, Ellie studied the face of the man she'd known since junior school. The man she'd thought – until the Christmas before last – she would grow old with. The delicate creases around his eyes. The slight twitching of his mouth. The speckles of grey around his temples.

It was the first time they'd been alone together since Dave's affair; since Ellie had asked him to leave and since she'd said she wanted a divorce; since Christmas when they'd started talking again. They'd chatted over the odd rushed coffee at the windmill with Zoe and Sylvia, but this was different.

And Ellie felt... what?

Heart rate up a little.

A bit nauseous.

'Did you *think* I would give up?'

'I didn't know.' She was dreading this conversation, aware it was likely to lead to questions about the future.

He shook his head decisively. 'I meant what I said at Christmas, Ells. I don't want to go back. I want us to move forward. If possible, *together*.' Dave kept his gaze on her for a few extra moments, as if needing to reassure himself that this was really happening; that Ellie was walking in the bluebell woods with him.

They entered the sheltered glade which led up to Rattling Folly. Shards of light shone on the bluebells, creating a violet glow.

'I know. But things are simpler for you. You had an affair. I can't push a button and all that trust magically comes back.'

'I understand that.' He stopped and turned to look at her. A pensive frown fell over his face. 'Tell me what I can do,' he said softly. 'How I can help. How can I convince you that I will never, ever, do that to you again?'

43

'That's the thing. I don't know.' The pain of what she said dug at her.

'Is it about forgiveness?'

Ellie thought a moment. 'A bit.' As they'd been talking, the knot of hurt still pulled in her abdomen.

Dave started walking again. 'I'll keep saying it then, over and over until you forgive me.' He spoke slowly. 'I'm really, really, sorry. It was a stupid, selfish mistake to start something with Andrea. I know I hurt you and I wish I could take it all back.'

'Thank you.' Ellie remembered the gym hall at primary school. She and Sally had a row and Dave was trying to cheer Ellie up. He had always been kind.

'I mean it. Please let me make it up to you?'

'It's not about that. It's not like missing someone's birthday. You can't buy me an outfit or a car or take me away on holiday and all the hurt disappears.'

'What, then?'

'Other than repeatedly saying that you made a mistake and wish you hadn't done it, I don't think there's anything else that you can say or do.' She stopped.

They were in front of Rattling Folly now.

Her hand joined his and for a few brief moments the two of them were suspended in time in their corner of the wood. Then she remembered Andrea and pulled her hand away.

'I don't know how to get rid of what I feel. I don't know if, in time, it will fade a little with every day. I know that you didn't do it deliberately to hurt me. But the problem is, for me, I still feel it in my body. If I think about you with Andrea, I feel sick. When you're near to me, or touch me, I want to pull you closer... *and* push you away. So, I don't think it's just about forgiveness. I think it's partly about hurt, and that I'm scared.'

Dave guided Ellie to a fallen log.

'Scared about what?'

Ellie gulped. Tears filled her eyes, as they always did when she thought about this. 'What you did destroyed my trust in you. We'd been together since sixth form. It never occurred to me in a million years that you might cheat on me.'

'Ellie.' His tone was pleading and full of pain.

They sat down.

'I'm scared you might—'

'I won't.'

'I don't want to get hurt again. I honestly don't know how I got through it. Before Christmas, you said we both have busy lives. That hasn't changed. You said you didn't feel like I loved you. Is that still the case?'

'No. It's not. I realised that you *do* love me. We both love each other. That's why I want us to get back together.' He paused. 'I take your point, though, that things are more complicated for you.'

'What if you get it into your head again that I don't love you? Are you then going to go and start an affair with someone else?'

Dave was shaking his head.

'That's the sticking point for me. You were able to do it with Andrea, so what's stopping you from doing it again?'

'I understand that. I really do.' Dave opened the picnic hamper. 'There's water or Sauvignon Blanc.'

'Wine, please.'

He took out glasses and a bottle. Olives, a crusty baguette, a camembert.

'Maybe it's just about time?' He poured out two glasses of wine and handed her one. 'And showing you that you can trust me?' He sipped his drink and sat in silence for a minute or two. 'Changing the subject, how's it going with my mother? Is she planning on going home in the foreseeable future?'

Ellie laughed. 'She's asked if she can stay on.'

Sylvia had arrived at the windmill before Christmas, when they'd had heavy snow for over a week, asking to stay for a few days – and still hadn't gone home.

'She's considering either renting her place out or selling it and moving to Wootton. Turns out she wasn't telling the truth when she said it was because she couldn't afford to heat her house—'

'I could've told you that.'

'There was an element of truth to it. The house *is* too big for her, and she is struggling to heat it and keep up with the maintenance. But what I didn't know was that Zoe had told her I was struggling.'

'Ah. You were "Zoe-ed".' Dave chuckled. 'That doesn't surprise me either.'

'To be fair, Zoe loves having her gran at home and I enjoy her company. And Sylvia seems to enjoy living with us so, really, it's win-win all round.'

'Are you still struggling? I know you were short of staff before Christmas. Are things better now?'

When Ellie kicked Dave out of the windmill eighteen months earlier, he'd said he was happy to continue sharing the bills but Ellie, in a fit of pride, had told him in no uncertain terms to stick his money. And while this made her feel better not to be reliant on him financially, it had put her under enormous strain, particularly when Zoe had fallen ill with glandular fever and wasn't able to work.

'I've taken on two more cleaners and your mother is helping in the office with the admin and book-keeping.'

'Thank goodness for that. You mentioned that you're losing customers though.'

She got up and ambled towards a nearby cluster of bluebells, filling him in with what had been happening.

'That sounds like business impersonation. Who is this other company?'

She crouched down, admiring the graceful bell shape of the flowers. 'I don't know yet. We are trying to find out. I have a feeling we'll need to review our prices. Modernise the business maybe.'

'Let me know if you need help. By the way, I know Mum really appreciates living with you guys. She misses Dad and values the company.'

'She enjoys being more involved with the kids.'

'I've seen a real change in her since she's been at the windmill,' Dave said. 'Thank you.'

Ellie laughed. 'You're only saying that because it gets you off the hook. Means you don't have to have her staying at your place.'

On one of the curving ash branches, a nuthatch tew-tew-ed.

'Sadly, that's very true.'

Ellie's phone pinged in her bag. It was probably Zoe, to see how their date – as she had insisted on calling it – was going.

Ellie took out her phone and swiped the screen. It was an unknown mobile number.

'That's strange.'

She clicked on the message.

'*Dave might be with you now, but do you know where he was last night and the night before? Ask him. If not, I can tell you. He was with me. Ruby.*'

'Oh, my goodness. What a—' A tremor shot through her hand.

'What's happened?' Dave was on his feet.

'It's your CSI colleague, Ruby.'

Dave kneeled on the ground beside her. '*Ruby?* Saying what?'

Ellie showed him the message.

Dave's face drained of colour as he read it.

In the distance, a wood pigeon coo-coo-ed.

'You see,' Ellie said. She took her phone back. 'This is exactly what I meant.'

'What she says isn't true,' he replied, placing his hand on his chest. 'I was not with Ruby last night or the night before, and I haven't been with her in a romantic way on any other night either.' He extended his hand. 'Let me see that again, please.'

Ellie screenshot the message quickly in case Dave was thinking about deleting it, and passed her phone back to him. 'Why would she send a message like this?'

'There can only be one reason. She wants to cause trouble between us. Leave it with me. I'll sort it out.' He glanced to the ground and Ellie caught the sweep of his eyelashes on his upper cheek. 'Please believe me. It isn't true.'

Ellie was swallowing down feelings of nausea. 'Has anything *ever* happened romantically between the two of you?'

'Nothing. Since Christmas, when I told you, she has continued to hint that she would like it to, but I have been clear with her that *that* is not what I want, and it isn't going to happen.' He got to his feet and walked towards the log. 'I have to liaise with the CSI team, but I've been very careful not to spend time with her outside work. In the past, for example, before I realised she... I've occasionally given her a lift but, since then, I've been very careful *not* to do that, and *not* to be alone with her under any circumstances except work.'

Ellie could see the tension in Dave's face. A muscle in his left cheek was twitching.

She wasn't sure what to think.

Did she believe him?

He hadn't told her about his affair with Andrea. She had only found out about it afterwards, and not from him. On the other hand, she hadn't asked him about it directly, as she had just done now with Ruby.

Her sense was that he was telling the truth.

So, why then did she have a sinking feeling in her stomach? Why was acid bubbling up? Was it because she knew something was happening between Dave and Ruby?

No.

How could she?

It was fear.

Plain old ugly fear.

This was why she could not possibly get back together with Dave now. Why she could not allow their relationship to veer into romantic realms. She *had* to make sure she kept things platonic and didn't open herself up to the possibility of being hurt again.

Her head throbbed at the temples.

'I'll talk to Ruby,' Dave said gently. 'I give you my word. I can't promise that she won't do anything like this again, but I will ask her not to.'

Ellie was nodding her head. 'I appreciate that. Part of me feels like going round to see her and explaining how it feels to be on the receiving end of a text message like that. But I don't want to wind her up. And I'm not going to reply to her message either.'

She took a slug of wine.

'Could we take a rain check on this evening, please?'

Dave covered his face with his hands. 'Please don't do this. Please don't let Ruby ruin the evening. It's taken me eighteen months to get you to agree to come out with me. Can't we just talk about... I don't know... Zoe, Mum, the windmill open day, work—'

'Sorry.'

Assuming Dave was telling the truth, it wasn't his fault that Ruby had sent Ellie the text message.

Nevertheless, the evening was over for her.

Chapter 8

6pm

As Ellie let herself in to the windmill, she knew there were going to be questions about why she was back early. She didn't know whether Zoe was at home, but as she walked up the front path she'd caught a glimpse of Sylvia through the window.

Ellie closed the front door. She buried her head briefly in Rebus' fur and said a quick hello to Sylvia who was in the kitchen, hoping to demonstrate by her body language that she didn't want to be put through the Spanish Inquisition.

'What are you doing back so early? Where's Dave?' Sylvia's face was full of concern.

'I'd rather not talk about it, if you don't mind. I'm going to go upstairs and have a bath.' Ellie caught Sylvia's sharp intake of breath as she hung up her jacket and deposited her bag on the kitchen table.

'If he has—'

'He hasn't done anything. Hopefully. Someone else has.'

Sylvia tipped her head sympathetically. 'You'll sort it out. I know you will. You climb in the bath, and I'll bring you up a nice cuppa and a pecan brownie. I've made a fresh batch for the open day. They've literally just come out of the oven. Finn and Zoe have wolfed one down already.'

'Gannets,' said Ellie, sniggering. 'Thank you. That would be gorgeous.' She slid upstairs and into the bathroom.

She turned the taps on full and watched as steaming water streamed into the roll top bath. She poured some lavender bath foam and inhaled the soothing aroma. Her mind was jangly with thoughts about Dave and Ruby, and she was desperate *not* to dwell on the realisation that she had been hoping she and Dave would get back together at some point.

While the water was running, she nipped into her bedroom and grabbed the paperback from by her bed. Hopefully, that would occupy her mind and stop her from picking at her frustration with her feelings.

She shut the bathroom door and a few moments later, was lying in the warm bubbly water reading about a woman who had walked a two-hundred-mile coastal path with her dog.

Sometime later, there was a knock downstairs at the front door. She heard Sylvia let the person in and greet them, then the sound of feet on the spiral staircase and a knock on the bathroom door.

'Ellie?'

She slid down under the bubbles, her reaction instinctive.

An image shot through her mind of Dave in bed with Andrea.

What was he doing here?

'I need to talk to you quickly. I'll go after that. Is it OK to come in?'

'Er... no. Sorry. What do you want?'

She didn't want him seeing her naked.

'I've been round to Ruby's.' He spoke through the door. 'Reiterated that nothing romantic is going to happen between her and me. Asked her to leave you alone.'

'OK. Thanks.'

'Apparently, she saw us walk across the green together. She'd had a bad day at work and knocked back a couple of glasses of wine. Basically, she was a bit tiddly and sent that message to you in a fit of jealousy.'

'OK. Thank you.' What else should she say? 'I'll see you soon.'

'I'll... er... go then, shall I?'

Tears rolled down Ellie's face. 'Yes, please.'

She lay motionless in the water, waiting for the sound of the front door. Then, when it came, she let out her breath and rested her head on the edge of the metal bath. Only hours earlier she'd been bubbling with excitement about her date with Dave. Now, hope had been snuffed out like an unwanted candle.

A few minutes later, her phone vibrated loudly.

Her heart sank.

Oh God. Please, don't let it be Ruby phoning now to add something else to her story.

Ellie glanced at the screen. It was Sally's number. She dried her hands, swooped up the phone in relief and swiped the screen. 'Sal?'

'Can you talk?' Her voice was jittery.

'Yeah sure. I'm in the bath but that's fine.'

'I thought you were having a picnic with Dave?'

'It ended earlier than expected. Anyway, what's up?'

'I'm really concerned. Pete's still not back. He texted, saying there was an *emergency*.'

'I take it you've rung him?'

'He's not answering his phone. I keep telling myself that maybe he's got the call volume turned down. But he's been gone ages and I can't stop thinking about that blood.'

Ellie closed her eyes briefly.

'What if the bow and arrow person has come after him?'

In the pub earlier, Ellie had felt that something odd was going on. Now she was sure of it.

'Whatever's happened, there's bound to be a good reason for it,' Ellie told her. 'Pete is Mr Sensible. I know it's a cliché but maybe the battery's gone flat on his phone. It does happen. Mine caught me out the other day. I must have used it a bit more than usual or left a load of apps open. Don't worry. He'll be fine.'

'I hope you're right. With Robert's death, I'm worried about Tracy, and I'm panicking that Pete might be involved.'

Ellie was thinking along the same lines but didn't want to add to her friend's anxiety.

The blood.

Pete's evasiveness.

'Could you make some inquiries? Please, Ells?'

Sally was her best mate.

Tracy was Sally's little sister. Tracy had put herself in danger to help Ellie. And now *she* needed help and Ellie owed her.

'OK. It's time for Blix Investigators to find out what's going on. I'll talk to Sylvia and Zoe and tell Tracy.'

'Thank you.'

'Goodness knows what I'm going to tell Dave though.' Ellie couldn't escape the feeling that this decision was going to cost her.

Chapter 9

7pm

Ellie was in her pyjamas and dressing gown in the lounge with Sylvia, Zoe and Finn. Rebus was on the sofa next to Ellie.

'Are we agreed that we'll investigate?' Ellie asked.

Sylvia and Zoe nodded.

'What about Dad?'

'I'll tell him I've changed my mind.' Ellie flicked open the Blix Blitz diary. 'OK, team. We need a plan. Let's decide who we are going to talk to tomorrow. Katie at the paper is on my list.'

'Yes, Katie, Pete, Tracy and Nick, the butcher,' Sylvia recited.

'Wow, Gran. You're on it this evening,' said Zoe, who was plaiting her hair.

'Just keen to get cracking.'

Ellie gestured to the diary. 'Zoe, you're at Mrs Henderson's from 9am to 10am tomorrow. She's washed all her curtains and needs a hand hanging them back up.' Ellie was scanning the day. 'Caroline's jobs are all sorted, same with Gill's and Alesha's.'

'Rightio,' Zoe replied.

'I think I'll go and see Katie first thing,' Ellie said. 'Try to find out who she got her information from.'

'Good luck with that.' Zoe snorted.

'I know,' Ellie replied. 'Got to try though... and check the time of death. Then I'll nip up to the garden centre. Ask Pete about the emergency and the clothes washing. And find out what he was up to before and after the wedding.'

'I'll go and ask Tracy about her phone,' Sylvia said. 'Then I'll pop into the butcher's and have a chat with Nick and Charlie Matthews about their burglary. Finn, perhaps you could come with me, given you know Charlie well?'

'No problem,' said Finn. 'Bob and I are cutting down Gladys Blackman's cherry tree tomorrow morning, but he'll be fine about me nipping off for half an hour if I tell him that it's to help Blix Investigators.'

'I suggest we go early, before the shop gets too busy,' said Sylvia.

'We can ask Nick what sort of archer we are looking for,' Finn added.

'That's a good idea.' Sylvia took the plastic off a new notepad. 'We aren't short of suspects, are we?' She turned to the first page and clicked on her biro. 'I started off wondering about Tracy, but I've got increasingly curious about Pete. Anyone else?'

'Same, Gran,' Zoe replied. 'But, talking about hotshot archers, I wouldn't mind betting that Tracy's ex-husband will have a motive.'

Chapter 10
DAY 2 - Friday, 7.30am

E llie usually started the day sitting down in the office at the windmill with Sylvia, checking on the Blix Blitz diary and making sure that all her cleaning staff were set. Now she had more employees, the business diary was more complicated and Ellie really appreciated Sylvia's help with not just the admin but the day-to-day running of the company.

Sylvia handed Ellie a mug of steaming tea.

Ellie dropped the calculator in disgust and took the mug.

Outside, the weather had changed and a spring shower was flinging itself against the brick base of the windmill.

'So far,' Ellie said, 'it's Gladys Blackman's house and the call centre in Dover who have given notice on their contracts. I've just totted up what it's going to cost the business. Based on their average invoices over the past twelve months, it currently works out at more than my increased salaries from taking on two new staff.'

'That's a lot of money,' Sylvia said.

'The call centre was a big payer. In two weeks, Blix Blitz will be back to where it was before Christmas.' Ellie took a slurp of tea.

It wasn't just the finances she was worried about.

Before Christmas, Ellie had been on her knees with exhaustion, and although it had been a temporary measure while Zoe was recovering from glandular fever, she had known that having to *do* the actual cleaning work as well as run the business was simply not sustainable for her, long term.

She couldn't go back to that.

She'd always enjoyed doing the physical work, but as she got older, her back, knees and hips were no longer up to cleaning all day, every day. The staff she employed were much younger than her. It didn't take the sort of toll on their bodies as it did on Ellie's.

'If only we knew why they were cancelling,' Sylvia said. 'At least then we might be able to do something about it.'

Ellie had a feeling something sneaky was going on. 'Before Christmas, I had too many contracts and too few

staff. Now I've got too many staff and not enough clients.'
She let out an exhausted sigh.

She really hoped today wouldn't bring more cancellations.

Because, unless things changed, she would have to lay off one of her new staff members – if not both – and go back to cleaning full-time.

She finished her tea and texted Sally, checking she was OK, and that Pete had got home safely.

Chapter 11

8.15am

Tracy's house was a mid-terrace at the end of Pennypot Lane. There were eight properties in her section, each painted a different pastel colour.

Sylvia liked the pretty primrose yellow of this one.

'Come in,' Tracy told her. 'Kieran and Emily are upstairs.' Her eyes brimmed with tears. 'It's all such a shock. I can't believe Robert is dead.' She paused, staring into space for a few moments. 'I feel... I don't know. I don't think I feel anything.'

'Take your time,' Sylvia replied. 'Feeling numb is a natural reaction. It's our brain's way of protecting us.' She knew about the stages of grief, and not just from her social work; she was still dealing with it after her husband's death.

'Angry. I'm really angry with that reporter for plastering Robert's death on the internet.'

Sylvia waited for Tracy to gather her thoughts.

'Thanks so much for helping us,' Tracy said.

'I have a few questions, if that's OK?' Sylvia flipped the pages of her notepad.

'Sure.'

'Do you have any idea how your phone could have ended up in the woods?'

'No. I lost it yesterday. I don't know where. Not sure if I dropped it or it was nicked.'

'Any idea what time?'

'Not really. I had a busy day and went from one thing to another. Into various shops, in and out of the car. Kieran had a Judo class and Emily had been on a sleepover.' She paused. 'I didn't realise that I didn't have it until I got home and went to text Sally.'

'Did you tell the police that you lost your phone yesterday?' Sylvia asked.

'Yes, I explained everything, but I didn't get the impression they believed me.'

'And you definitely weren't in the woods before the wedding and didn't drop your phone yourself?'

'No.' She was shaking her head. 'The kids and I were there for the wedding with everyone else. Before that we were at home. The thing is, when the police read the texts between Robert and me, it's going to increase their suspicions.'

'Oh dear. Why's that? You said yesterday that you haven't got on for a while.' Sylvia recalled Sally saying that she had been pleading with Tracy to divorce Robert.

'That was an understatement. You probably won't know this if you've only lived here for a few months. Around two years ago, Robert took over as manager at Wootton Farm Shop on the main road. The couple who owned it, Brian and Lily, have run it for years and they wanted to retire.'

'What happened?'

'Robert started doing all sorts of dodgy things which annoyed a lot of local people, things that weren't ethical and, from what I can gather, some things which were illegal.'

Sylvia sucked in a breath. 'Who did he annoy?'

'The two main people were Nick Matthews, the butcher, and Pete at the garden centre.'

Sylvia jotted a few notes. Good job they were seeing both men this morning.

'When I found out about what he'd been up to, I went mad. My sister and I have grown up in Wootton. The last thing I want is bad feeling with anyone in the village.'

Sylvia nodded.

'It was the last straw for me, and I told him I wanted a divorce. Around a year later, Brian and Lily terminated his contract and he left the shop in disgrace. A few weeks after that, he started a new job selling franchises.'

'Had he done sales before?'

'No. But the company offered training. When he got the new job, he begged me to give him another chance. Said he would make it up to me and show me he could be a better husband and father.'

What a difficult situation for Tracy.

It must have been very scary for her, wanting to split from a man she no longer trusted perhaps, and feeling... what? Obligated to give him another chance?

'And was he?'

'No. We had awful rows and he was violent a couple of times. He regularly bashed about in the house, slamming doors and breaking things.'

'Really sorry to hear that. You did tell the police this, didn't you?'

She nodded.

'What's the name of this franchise operation? Zoe is our tech expert. She can look them up.'

'BluePrint Franchises. They're based in Wincheap, near Canterbury. He was covering Essex, Kent, Sussex and Surrey, driving round, visiting potential customers.'

'That was some mileage.'

'Yes. He was often away for several days at a time because he said it was easier and saved money not to have to keep travelling home every night.'

'Where did he stay then?'

'In Travelodges and Premier Inns. With the cost of petrol, he worked out that it was cheaper to do that than to come home. Saved time on the road too.'

'Makes sense.'

'As far as I knew, Robert was away working yesterday. He wasn't due back 'til tomorrow.'

'He didn't say he was coming home early or coming to Wootton for any reason?'

'No.'

'It must have been quite a change for you all with him being away so much?' Sylvia asked.

'Definitely. The children missed him but, I'll give credit where it's due, he always made it up to them when he got home.'

'Did they get on well with him?'

'They adored him.'

'What about Liam? How did he get on with Robert?'

'Robert wasn't Liam's biological dad. Liam has always been closer to my ex-husband, Andy, than to Robert. From what I gather, that's quite common with divorces. He and Robert always seemed to jog along OK.'

'That's good. Separation is always complex,' Sylvia added, thinking about her social work cases.

'Liam has a lovely placid nature,' Tracy continued, looking reflective for a moment. 'He's always been easy-natured. I remember at school, nothing much seemed to faze him.'

'It probably helps that he's older than the other two.'

'Yes, he's had his own life for a few years now, so I don't think it bothered him when his dad and I split up.'

Sylvia wanted to check how Tracy was coping but before they moved on, she needed to ask about her ex-husband.

'How did Robert get on with Andy?'

'Andy hated Robert. He didn't want us to split up. He was very upset and angry, and thought that Robert had stolen me from him.'

They would need to add Andy to their suspect list.

'You moved on and got re-married. Has Andy not?'

'Liam told me he'd started going out with one of the stylists from the hairdresser in the high street. It didn't last long because... look, you'll need to ask him about that.'

'Do you think he hoped you and he would get back together?'

Tracy nodded. 'He knew it was unlikely, but I think he still hoped.'

'Oh, that's sad,' Sylvia said. 'Awful when a split is one-sided. It can be so painful. Especially when you have to watch the other person being happy with their new partner.' Could that have given Andy a motive for wanting Robert out of the way? They would need to speak to him. 'And you? How did you cope with Robert being away?'

'There was much more for me to do, obviously,' Tracy replied. 'I've got my part-time job and I have to do everything with the kids, get them to school, pick them up, but to be honest, Robert and I were arguing so much when he was at the farm shop, it's been a relief not to have that to contend with every day.'

'That must've been tough.'

'It was. And, although the kids missed him, it can't have been easy for them seeing us argue all the time either. They never said anything, but they took it all in, I know they did.'

'Sorry to ask this but have you got someone who can vouch for you yesterday morning, before the wedding?' Sylvia could see that Tracy had a lot of anger towards

Robert, and they couldn't afford to rule her out as a suspect.

'You mean an alibi?' Tracy replied. 'Yes. I was with the kids all morning and we went to the wedding together.'

'Was anyone else with you? Anyone see you or come round, for example, or ring you? It would be useful if someone other than the children could give you an alibi.'

Tracy was shaking her head. 'Don't think so.' A frown came over her features. Then relief. 'Oh, my sister, Sally. She came round to borrow some shoes for the wedding. She was in a bit of a flap because Pete was late getting home from the garden centre and she hadn't been able to get hold of him.'

'What time was that?'

'Around 9am yesterday morning.'

'That's OK then.'

Tracy let out a sob. 'It's so weird talking about Robert in the past tense. And in such matter-of-fact terms. It's all changed but we were very much in love when we got married.'

'Of course.'

'Relationships sour so easily, don't they? Our honeymoon phase wore off quickly, and it's been disillusionment ever since.'

'Very common,' said Sylvia. 'I saw it with a lot of my social work clients. Before I go, does your ex-husband still live locally? It must be nice that he and Liam see each other and get on well. Is it?'

'Andy lives just out of the village, near Priory Park. Yes, he and Liam have always been very close.'

It was time to leave Tracy in peace.

Given Ellie was going to see Pete, Sylvia needed to mention the dispute Robert had had with him over the farm shop. Although she suspected it was going to come out in Ellie's conversation... and probably a *lot* more.

Chapter 12

8.15am

When Ellie pulled off the drive into Pennypot Lane, Finn and Bob were on the village green. She beeped the horn and waved. Finn had started working for the local tree surgeon a few months earlier and the two had quickly become a great team. They were unloading the timber for the sheep pen for the open day at the windmill.

This fundraising event was the first of the year, with two more to come. Ellie's grandmother had introduced it and Ellie had kept the tradition going because it was popular. People travelled miles to see around the windmill and to imagine what it would be like to live in a circular building with three-hundred-and-sixty-degree views. They all enjoyed spending a few hours in the village, feasting on homemade cakes and taking part in traditional, rural activities.

Ellie felt a twinge of guilt.

Was it right to go ahead with what was essentially a celebration of their village when Robert's body was in the morgue?

As she drove through the village, her thoughts turned to her business and trying to solve the new issues it was facing. Dave continued to offer her help with the bills on the windmill, and Sylvia had offered to contribute too.

She might need to swallow her pride.

Before doing either of those things, though, she would think about ways of modernising Blix Blitz, of creating additional services to what they already offered and rewarding loyalty, the way every business seemed to do nowadays.

In the high street, the pink sun was high in the sky and locals were opening their businesses.

She passed the village hairdresser. Helen was putting the sandwich board outside listing the free appointments for the day. The Blixes were all customers. Helen's loyalty scheme didn't just offer a discount after the prescribed number of haircuts. It gave customers the option of a manicure, a pedicure or a facial, depending on how much money they'd spent. Perhaps Blix Blitz could do something similar?

Next, she passed the butcher's. Through the large shop window, she saw Charlie in the front, traying up meat. He had persuaded his dad to give regular customers a freebie of their choice each month. Sausages, chops, mince, chicken breasts. It wasn't as formal an arrangement as at the hairdresser's, but their customers appreciated it. The Blixes had all come home with free meat on occasions and a bone for Rebus several times.

It was just after eight when Ellie pulled into the garden centre, and the staff were opening up. The car park backed onto Appledown Woods and Pete was in the corner with another man, unloading heavy, brown, turf rolls from the back of a lorry.

Sally's voice came into her mind from the night before. What had the emergency been?

Pete was with Liam, Tracy's son. Ellie recognised him from the wedding and from when he had collected his mum from the windmill. She parked the jeep and got out, gathering her thoughts as she walked over to the lorry. 'Morning,' she said to them both. 'Really sorry about your stepfather,' she told Liam.

'Thank you. It's Mum I'm worried about.'

He had a warm, friendly manner.

Ellie wanted to talk to Pete about several things and one of those was Robert. 'Have you got a minute?' she said to him, hoping that he would ask Liam to start work on another job so that they could talk in private.

'Sure. Liam, buddy, do you want to go and give Fiona a hand inside with the stock? Everything got moved yesterday with all the water.'

'No problem.' Liam dusted off his hands and headed towards the entrance to the garden centre.

'Tracy has asked us to investigate Robert's murder and I wanted to ask you a few questions. First of all, though, Sally said you'd had an emergency last night. Is everything OK?' Ellie wondered if it was to do with the water he had just mentioned.

Pete stopped moving turf rolls and banged his hands together to brush off the soil. 'Yes. A pipe burst before the wedding and we had water everywhere in the shop. Masses of new stock damaged.'

Ellie gave a low whistle.

'I'm waiting for the loss adjuster. Called an emergency plumber first thing yesterday morning, as soon as I noticed it. That turned into a nightmare. Everyone was busy, just one guy who said he'd come and then took hours.'

'What bad luck with it being the day of the wedding. What did you do?'

'I didn't want to switch the water off at the mains because we've got fishponds with waterfalls, and any changes can affect the fish.'

'Of course.'

'So, I rang round to see who could help me. The only people in the village who have plumbing experience are Charlie Matthews and Robert Seale.'

'*Robert?*'

'Yes. He used to work for a plumber's business before he took over the farm shop. Fell out with the governor, I gather, and, like everything else with him, he just moved on to something different.'

'Who did you get to help?'

'Nick. Charlie was out but he suggested I ask his old man. Linda is super-organised and had got their wedding clothes out the night before. All Nick needed to do was get changed.'

'Was he able to come straight over?'

He nodded. 'I'll show you the damage.' He began walking towards the front entrance of the garden centre and Ellie followed.

It was a large, single storey warehouse-style building with a corrugated iron roof.

Inside, it was open plan and the entrance brought them into the checkout area of the shop. Here, four cash desks stood next to each other. Along the front wall, shopping baskets had been stacked, small ones and larger ones on wheels with a long handle.

In one corner, Ellie saw a café with tables and chairs, counters with display cabinets, coffee machines. She waved at a couple from the village who were sipping coffee and looking at seed packets.

'Thankfully, the leak hasn't affected the café, and all of the sockets worked when we switched the power back on. It *has* affected a lot of stock though. We will get the money back from the insurers, eventually, but you know what they're like. They make you jump through hoops and the loss adjusters always down-value the damage.' Pete pointed to an area which had been cleared of garden furniture. Sun loungers, benches, outdoor tables were stacked on top of each other. 'All new stock. Only came in a few days ago.'

'Such bad luck. I had no idea. Will you be able to keep trading like this?'

'I've made sure we aren't contravening any health and safety laws, so we should be OK as long as we can keep the income coming in. As far as I can gather, it basically means us ensuring that the area is safe.'

Ellie could see how much work they had done.

'We've taped off the area of damage so no customers can enter and have made sure that the leak is properly fixed. It's up to the loss adjuster from here.'

'I see what you mean. Do you know what caused it?'

'Not for definite.' He hesitated. 'I mean, the flexi pipe was rusted and gave way, but whether that happened on its own, I have my doubts. We traced the pipe from the break to the tap outside.'

Ellie was thinking about what Sally had said about Pete's clothes. She had described the mess on Pete's boots as being like the mud in the woods. And full of leaves.

'Could you show me the outside area?'

Pete frowned. 'Sure, but there's not much to see, just a tap really. Most of the mud has gone now that the water has been absorbed into the ground.'

'Thank you.' Ellie followed Pete around the side of the building to the back.

Here, there was more stock. Bags of peat, compost, fertiliser, stones, sand and a tap.

But Ellie couldn't see a single tree which could account for the leaves on Pete's boots.

'Thank goodness it's all dried up. What an awful palaver for you, and at a really rubbish time.' She began tracing their steps back round to the entrance. 'Sally also mentioned you did some washing. Presumably, that was to do with the water leak. And that you'd cleaned leaves off your boots.' The last bit was a lie.

Pete flinched when she said 'leaves' and began looking about as though hoping he might find some on the ground.

Chapter 13

8.45am

When Sylvia and Finn arrived at the butcher's in the village, the chalk boards were already out on the pavement, leaning up against the shop front, advertising special offers, new arrivals and deals of the day. A string of colourful bunting ran across the shop window. Charlie Matthews had learnt his trade from his father and was serving customers at the counter. In his white coat, his black spiky hair was striking.

The Matthews ran their business the old-fashioned way. No polystyrene or cling film or dodgy sell-by dates. They cut up locally sourced meat each morning before the shop opened and arranged it in metal trays in large chiller cabinets. On the counter, an honesty box lay in a basket of free-range eggs.

'Alright, mate?' Charlie greeted Finn. 'Mrs Blix?'

'Is your old man around?' Finn replied. 'Zoe's Gran wanted to have a quick word with him about the burglary at your place?'

Charlie handed a few bags of meat to one of the village mums, who was standing next to Sylvia and Finn. She took her change from Charlie and stowed her purchases into her trolley bag. 'First the break-in, now this poor man's murder,' she said, fixing her attention on Sylvia, as though she had the answers.

'It is a worry, isn't it?' Sylvia replied. 'I'm sure both will be solved soon.'

'Dad, Mrs Blix Senior is here to see you.' Charlie shouted over his shoulder.

'Less of the "senior", thank you very much,' Sylvia replied, chuckling. It was a standing joke between them, one neither seemed to tire of.

Nick appeared in the doorway into the back shop. Same white coat and dark hair as his son but stockier and with grey at the temples.

Sylvia didn't like to tell him that she always remembered him in shorts and an aertex top at sports day with Ellie and Dave. Since moving back to Wootton, she was still getting used to how far back families in the village went.

'Sure. I'm checking the fridge temperatures but I'm more than happy to stop for a minute.'

Sylvia and Finn walked behind the counter.

'Sorry to disturb you when you're busy.'

'Not at all. Always time for Dave's mum. Come on through.'

'It's my fault that we're here,' said Finn. 'I remembered that some of your archery equipment was stolen in the burglary. Mentioned it at home and—'

'...the Blix women are investigating,' Nick said. 'That's absolutely fine. I'm more than happy to answer any questions.'

'I take it that what Finn said is true, then?' Sylvia asked. 'You did have bows and arrows taken?'

'We certainly did. One of mine and one of Charlie's.'

'Sorry to hear about the burglary. I do hope you weren't in when it happened?'

'Fortunately, we weren't. We were away for the weekend and Charlie doesn't live at home anymore.'

'I have to say I rather wish I'd been at home, because they got away with my favourite bow. It's the one I was planning to use for the archery demonstration at the open day on Sunday.'

'That's a shame. Let's hope the police recover it.' Sylvia opened her notepad. 'Now, I don't know anything about archery. Can we start with whether one of the bows you had stolen could have been used to shoot the kind of arrow that Robert was killed with.'

'I haven't seen the arrow so I can't say for certain whether it was one of ours or whether it could have been fired from either of our bows, but from what I've heard, it sounds likely. And it's a bit of a coincidence if it isn't.'

'Exactly. That's why we thought it would be a good idea to talk to you. Now, it looks like the arrow in Robert's back killed him so—'

'The police have been in,' Nick said. 'He was definitely killed by that one shot.'

That was a handy piece of information.

'In your experience, is it quite common for arrows to be that deadly?'

'Oh yes. There are lots of myths about archery and whether or not someone could die from an arrow wound. There are two schools of thought, neither of which is completely accurate. Both stem from films and television, in my opinion.' Nick moved a set of scales.

Sylvia perched on a stool, relieved she was wearing stretchy jeans. She had never seen so many refrigerators. The back room was wall-to-wall fridges, all floor-to-ceiling and gleaming steel.

'The first is that arrows are simply slightly longer versions of darts and are therefore pretty harmless,' Nick continued. 'The second is the one portrayed in films where you have an exhausted hero hanging by one arm off a tree, shooting an arrow with the other and killing the person dead with one perfect shot.' He laughed.

'I know the type of scene you're talking about.' Zoe and Finn had recently persuaded her and Ellie to watch one of their fantasy series on Netflix, and it had been just as Nick described.

'The truth is, they are lethal weapons in the *wrong* hands or the *wrong* situation. However, it's not just about the type of arrow. Sure, that will have a big influence on the wound caused but there are other important factors too, predominantly the skill of the archer. Their strength isn't so crucial these days.'

'Why is that?' Finn asked, following every word.

'A lot of the new bows don't require much strength. The mechanics of the weapon do all the work.'

'And the deadliness?'

Nick was cleaning his knives and stowing them in the rack. 'When an arrow goes into a chest cavity, it has the potential to go into both the heart and the lungs. Depending on the kind of arrow used, this sort of wound can do a lot of damage. If first aid isn't received almost immediately, it's very likely to result in death. From what

I gathered from the police, this is what happened with Robert.'

'Is there quite a bit of skill involved in that sort of shot?' Finn asked. 'I'm hoping Charlie will teach me archery one day.'

'From what I've heard, Robert only had one arrow in the centre of his back. The most likely scenario is that whoever did it took one shot and hit their target. That takes skill, experience and practice. Unless the person was aiming for a completely different part of the body and missed.'

'That's very useful, thank you,' Sylvia said.

'I would add,' Nick said, 'that a bow and arrow are what's called "ranged weapons". In other words, the arrow is propelled further than a normal throw will achieve.'

Finn leaned forward in interest.

'This gives the archer a number of attack advantages.'

'I'm guessing these are that they can shoot from behind, from the air or from a distance?' Finn said.

'Very clever,' Sylvia added. 'I was wondering why the killer might use a bow and arrow. It's hardly inconspicuous. But if you can shoot from a distance, you can conceal yourself.'

'Exactly,' said Nick.

'It looks like Robert wasn't given any help and was left to die,' Sylvia said. 'It seems likely that this was the archer's intention.'

She couldn't help thinking about the fact that Robert was meant to be away working and not in Lower Wootton at all until today.

How, then, had he ended up dead in the woods? Had he been lured there? And, if so, by whom?

'It's tragic,' Nick said. 'I can't imagine how Tracy and the kids must be feeling. Horrific for them.'

'My next question is – who in the village has archery experience and skill?'

'Well, experience and skill aren't the same thing, of course. Charlie and I run an archery club in the village, which is meant to be for children and teens, but half the parents ask to join too.'

'I can imagine,' Sylvia said. 'I'm tempted to ask if *I* can join. I need a new interest.'

'They're what I call hobbyist archers. The more serious ones tend to join a range.'

'Are there many of them round here?' Finn asked.

'There are several, not just the one that we go to in Deal. There's one in Sandwich and one in Eybridge.' He turned back to Sylvia. 'But to answer your question... let me see now. Your Dave has been to the range with us a few times.

He's very good actually. Pete came a few years ago, but the garden centre is so busy these days I don't think he gets time to do much else.'

Sylvia was jotting on her notepad. 'Is it possible that a woman could have shot the arrow that killed Robert?'

'Definitely. Modern bows don't require much strength.'

'Just a couple more things I wanted to ask you about, if that's OK?'

'Fire away.'

'I gather you and Robert came to blows over the farm shop a while back. Could you tell me a bit about that, please?'

Nick's story was similar to what Tracy had said earlier. Robert had ignored the agreement between the Matthews' and the farm shop that the latter wouldn't sell meat.

'When I confronted Robert, he got physical. He was a strong chap and taller than me. He got hold of my jacket and bundled me out of the shop.'

'That's a terrible way to behave,' Sylvia said.

'I've never liked the bloke, but he crossed a line that day. Not just with the meat but with how he behaved when I tried to speak to him about it.'

Sylvia's social work radar dinged. She had met a lot of men who, like Robert, had no compunction about behaving aggressively with people in their community and alienating other business owners. They often showed traits of psychopathy.

'How did you leave things with Robert? He threw you out of the shop and...?'

'... and I told him that he wouldn't get away with it.' Nick's voice shook as he spoke.

Sylvia caught the anger in his words. 'What did you mean by that? It could be seen as some kind of threat.'

'I suppose it was... but I wasn't thinking about shooting him in the back with a bow and arrow, if that's what you're thinking. What I meant was that his actions had cost me a lot of money and I intended to pursue that legally.'

'When was the last time you saw him?'

Nick frowned. 'Er, I'm not sure. I've probably seen him around the village.'

Sylvia was aware that Finn was watching Nick closely too. 'You didn't, for example, see him or speak to him yesterday morning before the wedding?'

'I did *not*.' There was a hint of irritation in his reply.

'OK, thanks.' Sylvia wasn't convinced this was the full story. They would need to do some more digging. 'The other thing I wanted to ask you about was you helping Pete at the garden centre yesterday.' Sylvia deliberately didn't repeat what Sally had told them as she wanted to see what Nick would say.

A pipe burst. Difficulty finding a plumber. 'I helped Pete mop up all the water from the floor and move as much stock as we could so that it didn't get damaged. He's been remarkably stoic about it all, much more so than I would have been if it had been this place. I just hope the insurance company pay up and don't start messing him around.'

He confirmed he'd helped Pete before the wedding and afterwards.

'He was understandably anxious about leaving the place and going to the wedding. He thought the plumber might turn up and then disappear again when he saw that nobody was there.'

Sylvia groaned. 'That always happens, doesn't it?'

'Yes. But Pete wanted to get to the wedding and not let Adrian and Jane down, so he rang the plumber and told him to call when he was on his way. In the end, the wedding finished before the chap arrived. We went to check on the pipe and to make sure that everything was OK.'

'And was it?'

'No, unfortunately. We thought we had got rid of all of the water, but we hadn't, and when we got back a lot more of the stock had been damaged than we initially thought.' He confirmed they were at the garden centre until around midnight, mopping up and wiping down stock.

'Thanks, Nick,' said Finn. 'You've been ace.'

'Yes,' Sylvia added. 'Very generous with your time and explained things fully. I think we all hope that Robert's killer is caught as quickly as possible.'

'It's awful for his family,' Nick replied, 'and hasn't, I'm sure, created the best wedding experience for Adrian and Jane either. I gather they're holding their reception on Sunday evening now, after the open day.'

'I'll make sure Ellie knows,' Sylvia said. 'It's all very well agreeing to help find out what happened but it's not pleasant having to ask friends in the village where they've been and why, and who they've been with.'

'It's harder when people have had a ruck,' Finn said. 'I remember when the Blixes investigated my mum's death.' He gestured to Sylvia. 'Ellie and Mum had fallen out at school. Then loads of people saw them rowing just before Mum was killed.'

Nick nodded. He reached into one of the fridges and produced a large bone. He bagged it up and passed it to Sylvia. 'For Rebus.'

'Thank you. He'll love that.' Sylvia deposited the package on the counter.

'You know, I remember Tracy from school,' Nick said. 'Ellie, Dave, Sally, Pete, Andrea. We were all in the same year. I think Tracy was a few years younger than us, but because she was Sally's sister, we all got to know her too.'

'Speaking of Tracy – could I check something with you? She said her ex-husband is a good archer. Is that true, do you know?'

'Those two got into archery through our kids' club. They brought Liam along.' He laughed. 'Andy's not bad. But Tracy's being a bit coy there. Andy's archery isn't a patch on hers. Used to drive him mad when she beat him.'

Sylvia stared at Finn. 'Tracy does archery?'

'She *did*. She and Andy used to go to the range in Sandwich. Big, posh place, it is. Whether she's kept it up or not, I don't know.'

Something else that Tracy hadn't told them.

Chapter 14

8.30am

Pete and Ellie were still discussing the water leak at the garden centre.

'Don't know anything about leaves,' Pete told Ellie. 'But I ended up drenched and caked in mud. And had rust from the flexi pipe all over my clothes.' He looked down as though expecting it to still be there. 'Rather than leave it all to dry, when I got home, I took my clothes off and chucked them in the washing machine.'

'Makes sense.' Ellie knew that rust often looked like blood when it dried. One of her cleaners had got it wrong once on a client's laundry.

'It probably seemed odd because I don't usually do that. I'm sure Sal's told you. I'm a bit anal about the environment and do full loads of whites and colours separately.'

'So, did you sort the leak out, go to the wedding and come back?'

When Ellie was in the bath, Sally had said Pete still wasn't home.

'Exactly that. In the end, we were forced to switch the water off at the mains. After the wedding, I came back here to check on things. The emergency plumber didn't arrive 'til around 10pm and was here until around midnight. Sally was asleep by the time I got home. Or at least I think she was.'

'Sally mentioned that you and Robert had a text message exchange the other night when you were watching a film.' Ellie wanted Pete to be honest with her. They had all been friends since school days and Ellie wasn't comfortable with trying to trap him.

Pete nodded his head slowly. 'That's correct. We did. He owes me money and it's gone on long enough. He needs to pay up. Well, obviously it's too late now but that was what I was suggesting in my texts to him.'

'And what was his answer?'

'First of all, he tried to pretend that he had paid me. Then he claimed he had forgotten that he *hadn't*, and when I asked him for the money, he then said he didn't have it.'

'That's quite a shift within one conversation.'

'Tell me about it. It was always the same with him. He was quite the Houdini. It's very unusual for me to actually dislike someone but I can honestly say, hands up, I really did not like Robert. He was a lying, cheating scumbag.'

'Where did you leave things with him?'

'I told him I wanted the money in full by the end of the month. He carried on saying that he didn't have it, that he'd have to get a loan or something, and I said I didn't care.'

Questions were forming in Ellie's mind.

If Robert said he didn't have the money and Pete said he would have to find it, that didn't sound like a solution.

'Did you leave it there? I mean, a situation like that usually ends with an ultimatum.'

Pete frowned.

'What I mean is, after "You've got to", there's no real response except, "Make me then".'

'You surely don't think I had anything to do with Robert's murder?'

Ellie had to be honest.

'Knowing you as I do, I think it's highly unlikely, but Sally and Tracy have asked Sylvia, Zoe and me to look into his death.'

'I obviously said that it wasn't OK and he stated – like he always did – that it was tough. I'd have to lump it.' He was shaking his head in frustration, as though he still couldn't understand how someone could be so difficult, why they would want to be. 'I said I wasn't going to, I'd had enough, I wanted my money, but he just repeated like a broken record that he didn't have it and wasn't going to pay.'

Ellie felt Pete's exasperation.

'Like you say, if someone refuses to pay up, you only have a limited number of options. Although I felt like it, I wasn't about to frogmarch him down to the bank and stand over him while he made a withdrawal.'

It seemed strange to Ellie, again, that Pete hadn't told Sally what the debt was about. 'What did he owe you money for?'

'You know what happened with the farm shop, right?'

'Not the details. Only that Robert made a mess of things.'

'There was much more to it than that. The people who owned the farm shop before he took over never sold or supplied Christmas trees. We had a gentlemen's agreement that this was something I would do. But when Robert took over, he blew all of that up. He started selling individual trees, which was annoying enough, and he also started supplying some of the places that I supply. I had ordered the stock, ready to sell, and then wasn't able to because

Robert had undercut me. I couldn't return the trees either, so I had to pay for them.'

'What an awful way to behave.'

'Robert was aware what he was doing was wrong. He knew all about the agreement, but, of course, he lied and pretended he didn't. I told him that I was going to take him to court for my financial losses. At that point, he suddenly remembered that he had known all along about the arrangement.'

Ellie was shocked.

'He begged me not to take him to court and I agreed, as long as he reimbursed me for the loss. I showed him all the receipts. I added them up in front of him. He knew what the total was. Over two thousand pounds. So, there you have it. That's what he owed me.'

Ellie was processing the information.

What else did she want to ask him?

'You definitely didn't go into the woods to meet Robert or anyone else? Either before or after Robert was killed?'

An unreadable expression flashed across Pete's face.

Was it irritation or something else?

'On both occasions I was here at the garden centre,' said Pete, and Ellie noticed he hadn't denied going into the woods. 'Nick can vouch for me.'

'Before the wedding or after?'

'Both. Nick gave me a hand afterwards too.'

Ellie was sifting through Pete's testimony.

He made it sound very logical but, when she listened to him, she got the same feeling as she had done when he had been talking about the washing machine.

That it wasn't the truth.

Ellie thought of Liam, Tracy's son. 'Shame Liam couldn't have helped you. He seems quite handy.'

'He's very handy. An excellent worker. Good with the customers too. The oldies adore him. He jokes away with them and teases them and carries their stuff to the car. But after the wedding he and Charlie took off.'

'That was bad luck.'

'The only downside with Liam is that wherever he goes, Andy Morris turns up.'

'Really? For what reason?'

'I don't know if he's checking up on Liam or on the people he's with. It got worse when he and Tracy split up.'

Ellie remembered what Sally had said about Andy not wanting the split. Perhaps he was worried about losing Liam too?

'I've had to have a word with Andy. Ask if he can stop dropping by here. He scares the customers.'

'Doing what?'

'I don't know if it's his weight training physique... or his booming voice...'

'When was the last time that happened?'

'Yesterday. He was here when I arrived in the morning, waiting for Liam.'

'What time was that?'

'I got here at 7.30am and he was already here, stuffing a bacon sarnie. Think he'd been walking the dog in the woods.' Nick gestured over his shoulder to Appledown Woods.

'What did he want?'

'Don't know. They had a brief conversation and Andy left.'

Ideas shot through Ellie's mind. 'But Liam isn't scared of his dad, is he?'

'Oh, no. But Liam is very placid. Nothing seems to rattle him. I've literally never seen him get annoyed.'

Ellie's thoughts shifted to Sally. If she hadn't known where Pete was, before and after the wedding, did she also not know about the flood here at the garden centre? 'Sorry if it sounds nosy but we have all known each other since school – have you told Sally about the flood?'

'I haven't yet. I didn't want to worry her.'

'She loves you and cares about you, you doughnut. She would want to help.'

He shrugged. 'I suppose I felt a bit embarrassed. I lost money over the Christmas trees and now I'm facing an insurance claim which will be in the tens of thousands.'

'But she didn't know where you were. And then you said there was an emergency.'

'I didn't want her worrying unnecessarily. What did she think I was up to, then?'

'I don't think she knew, that was the problem. A local has been killed. I think all our imaginations are running wild.'

Pete was nodding.

Ellie was worried that it sounded like she was either being nosy or a bit judgmental and telling Pete off. Sally was her best friend, but she was very fond of Pete too. At the same time, Ellie couldn't shake the feeling that something wasn't quite right about what Pete was telling her.

'Anyhow, I will leave it to you to tell Sally what you want. Just to be crystal clear, though, are you saying that you do not know *anything* about Robert's death? That you didn't see him yesterday morning at all?'

Pete looked Ellie in the eye. 'I can say quite categorically that I don't know anything about Robert's death.'

Ellie noticed that Pete hadn't answered her second question.

She couldn't get the leaves out of her mind. What if Pete had been in the woods and seen or heard something? And didn't want to say?

She was finding it hard to square the Pete she knew and loved from primary school, secondary school and sixth form with the person in front of her now.

'Please tell me the truth. Did you see Robert yesterday morning or have a conversation with him?'

'I did not.'

Try as Ellie might, it shook her to the core to even think that her childhood friend, her best friend's boyfriend, was lying to her.

Chapter 15

9am

Ellie hadn't been to the *Wootton Gazette* offices for over a year and when she arrived, she got a shock. The beautiful old red brick building just outside Deal had been knocked down and replaced by a glass monstrosity of the same height. As she approached in the glorious spring sunshine, light reflected off the glass and caused her to squint.

She wasn't in the mood for Katie Douglas.

But – that was tough.

She was going to have to pull her big girl knickers on and get on with it.

She had rung ahead to check if Katie was in the office, saying she had a document to drop off for her in person. Katie was going to be there, she was told, until mid-morning.

Ellie parked the jeep on the roadside. She took out her phone and brought up Katie's newspaper article.

'Early hours' was how she had described when Robert had been killed.

She stuffed her phone in her pocket and headed for the entrance. She was a hundred yards or so away when she saw Tracy striding down the path towards her.

What was Tracy doing at the local paper? Hadn't she asked the Blixes to investigate Robert's murder on her behalf?

'Ellie?'

'Hi,' Ellie replied. 'What are you doing here? Sylvia was going round to see you.'

Tracy blushed. 'She's been and gone. I was so mad about Katie's article, I decided I wanted to speak to her myself.'

That didn't ring true.

'What did she have to say?'

'Not much... you know what she's like, as evasive as anything.'

'Did she tell you who her informant was?'

'Did she, heck. She waffled on about protecting her sources and making sure that she didn't put anyone in danger.'

'That woman is such a hypocrite. She publishes information highly sensitive in a new murder investigation and expects us to believe that's not putting anyone in danger?'

'Exactly. But you know what she's like.'

'Did you get anything useful out of her at all?'

'Not really.'

As Tracy spoke, Ellie couldn't help wondering whether she was telling the truth. It was, of course, perfectly conceivable that Katie would have said the exact things that Tracy was reporting. But it had been obvious when she and Sylvia were talking to Tracy that she was struggling to cope. It seemed odd that she would go and confront Katie when she knew the Blixes were on the case.

'Well, I guess I'll have a go then. See if I can get any more information out of her.' She paused, still wondering what Tracy had come for. 'It's all changed since I was last here. Very posh. What is Katie's office like? I always get lost in these places. They're like a maze.'

'It's all open plan. No privacy at all. I'm quite sure everyone heard every word I said.' Tracy glanced off to the side. 'Anyway, let me know how you get on. Hopefully you'll have better luck than me.'

The two women said goodbye and Ellie continued towards the entrance.

Once inside, she headed for the swanky wooden reception desk, taking in the lobby as she walked. Security guard. Water cooler. Spread of newspapers on a glass table, next to an enormous vase full of exotic flowers with long stems.

Weren't local newspapers struggling for income? And constantly complaining about free content on the internet? She didn't get the impression that whoever was in charge here was struggling to balance the books.

'Hey Mrs Blix. Can I help you?' A pretty girl in her twenties was smiling at Ellie. It was Roxie, daughter of Helen from the village hair salon.

'Hi. Yes. I'm here to drop off something for Katie Douglas. She's asked me to bring it in for her. Could I nip up and see her? I know where her office is.' She would have to ask someone for directions once she got round the corner.

'Sure.'

'Don't bother to buzz through. She knows I'm on my way.'

'No problem.'

Ellie felt a pang of guilt for lying. However, a man had been murdered and the local paper was publishing irresponsible information. She scuttled off before Roxie changed her mind.

Once Ellie got round the corner she was faced with the lifts. There was nowhere else to go but she didn't know which floor Katie's office was on. Should she wait for someone to come out of the lift and ask for directions? If she did that, she'd run the risk of being confronted about what she was doing, or, God forbid, even bumping into Katie herself.

The lifts at the call centre in Dover had handy descriptors next to the control panel. Hopefully, these would too.

She pressed the button to open the lift doors and strode inside. She could always go to each floor in turn and ask for directions there. But, as luck would have it, there was a sign saying which department was on which floor. Ellie pressed the button for the news room. The lift whirred smoothly into action and moments later she was stepping out into an open plan office on the second floor.

Perhaps she had been wrong about Tracy after all.

Ellie pulled a friendly, slightly vague expression onto her face and wandered over to the first desk that she saw. 'Hi. I'm dropping something off for Katie,' she said to a young man who was bashing away at a keyboard. 'Which is her desk, please?'

He raised his gaze and pushed his black rimmed glasses up the bridge of his nose. 'She's in the office next to the editor's, along the left-hand wall over there, the second one as you go past. The first is Harry's. The next one is Katie's.'

'Brilliant. Thanks.'

She strode along the side of the office, trying her best to look as if she knew exactly where she was going. As she approached the first office, she lengthened her stride, hoping that she wouldn't crash into the glass walls round Katie's when she tried to turn. Cleaning people's houses was a world away from this kind of subterfuge.

Fortunately, the door to Katie's office was open and Ellie walked in, her body at a slight angle from negotiating the corner at speed. 'Morning. Could I have a word?' She straightened up.

'Ellie Blix. What are you doing here? How did you get in?' Katie was in a large leather chair, hair a deeper cherry than last time they'd met.

'I wanted to ask you about the article you wrote in the newspaper about Robert Seale's death.' She rattled off her question before Katie got the chance to shut her down. 'Where did you get your information from? The police still haven't released to the public half of the details that you shared.'

Katie sat back in her leather chair and laughed loudly. 'You don't really think I'm going to tell you that, do you? I'm getting a strong sense of déjà vu here.'

'Well, I can always hope.'

'Don't tell me you and your fellow amateurs have got your sleuthing fingers on this one too?'

'We have indeed. In fact, it was Tracy who asked us to investigate.'

A frown crossed Katie's brow and for a moment, Ellie wondered whether Tracy had been to speak to Katie at all.

Time of death. Ask Katie about the time of death.

'In your article, you wrote that Robert was killed in the early hours of yesterday. You do realise, don't you, that your *source* has given you the wrong information?'

Katie pursed her beautifully lip-sticked mouth. 'You what?'

'Unless, of course, you deliberately wrote incorrect information?'

She had to bite, surely?

'It was not incorrect. That is exactly what they said.'

Ellie noticed the use of 'they'. That was fine. Ellie would use it too. 'But it wasn't the early hours, was it?'

Katie leaned over her desk and Ellie could see her thinking.

There was no way the police would have given this information to Katie at that early stage, when they weren't telling anybody what the time of death had been.

It meant that Ellie could refer to the police and Katie wouldn't be able to say categorically whether it was true or not.

'Ah. Got it. You're trying to trick me again, aren't you? I'm not falling for it this time. Although, I have to say, it did give me immense pleasure to write about that useless, philandering, ex-husband of yours before Christmas. You'll need to try harder.'

'I don't have to try anything. I'm simply giving you the official facts,' she lied. 'He *wasn't* killed in the early hours. He was killed at 9am. Either your source has *deliberately* given you wrong information or they don't know what they're talking about.'

Katie snorted. 'I think it's far more likely that *your* source has the wrong information because I can tell you without a shadow of doubt that Robert was killed at 5am, not 9am.'

Bingo.

She'd confirmed the time.

Don't react. You don't want her knowing you've tricked her again. Just move on.

'Well one of us is right. I guess we'll soon find out.'

Now ask your next question. Be super reasonable.

'Katie, if you know who the killer is, you've got to tell the police. What if they're out there somewhere, planning their next murder? If you don't want to tell *me* who your source is, that's fine, but at least tell the police so they can interview them.'

'Except that wouldn't be protecting my source, would it? No one is going to tell me anything if I start dobbing them in to the police.'

'Is your source Robert's murderer? Please tell me that it isn't.'

'It isn't.'

'Touché.' Ellie tried to gather her thoughts. She wanted to tell Katie that what she was doing was unethical but it was pointless. 'Does Harry know about this? Your secret source?'

'All sources are secret, Ellie.'

'Does he know you've published information the police haven't released yet?'

'What do you think, Miss Marple? He's the editor of the paper.'

Ellie was wasting her time hoping to get any more out of Katie, and it seemed unlikely that she would have better luck next door with Harry. She had, however, found out the time of death and that was going to be incredibly useful. What Katie had done was wrong, but the Blix women would find out who murdered Robert.

'Fair enough. Can I, please, ask you again to share the person's identity with the police? This isn't a game, reporting on murders. Robert has left a wife and young children behind.'

'Sorry. No can do. Now – if that's it, I really need to get on. Shall I walk you back to the lift or do you think you could manage it on your own?'

Ellie had one final question. 'Have you considered why anyone in their right mind would give you the sort of information that they have? What on earth were they hoping to achieve? Their ten minutes of fame? Some bizarre satisfaction from knowing that they were interfering with a police investigation?'

'I just write the stories. It's not my job to worry about why people tell us about things that have happened. That's their look-out.' Katie stood up behind her desk. 'Now, I need to get on.'

'Before I go, did Tracy leave her scarf in here?' Ellie pretended to look round Katie's office.

'I haven't seen Tracy. Why would her scarf be in here?'

Chapter 16

9.30am

The discussion with Katie Douglas sent questions and ideas darting through Ellie's mind as she walked through the *Gazette* newsroom to the lifts.

Robert had been killed at 5am.

How many people would have been able to get themselves into the woods that early in the morning, with a bow and arrow, without someone in their family knowing?

As she went down in the lift, she wondered why Tracy had been at the *Gazette's* offices, why she said she had been to see Katie when she hadn't, and who, therefore, she had been to see.

As the adrenaline began to subside, a cold shiver crept over Ellie. It had been Tracy who had asked them to look into Robert's death before Sally mentioned it. She was

Ellie's best friend's sister and Ellie had been happy to help. But now she felt distinctly uncomfortable knowing that, for whatever her reasons, Tracy had lied to her outside the offices around half an hour ago.

The second lie she had told them.

Once Ellie was back in the fresh air, she took her phone out of her bag and brought up the landline number at the windmill. She pressed 'dial' and carried on walking towards the car.

Sylvia took ages to answer. 'Blix Investigators.' She was out of breath.

Ellie chuckled. 'That's going to confuse the cleaning customers. They'll think we've turned into a private detective agency.'

'Your number came up on the display. Sorry... just back from the butcher's...'

'According to Katie, Robert was killed at 5am,' Ellie told her.

'That is going to rule out a *lot* of people.'

'And Pete told me earlier that when he arrived at the garden centre yesterday morning, Andy Morris was there. He'd been walking the dog in the woods.'

'That could put him on the spot at the right time,' Sylvia said.

'Exactly.'

'And Tracy has just lied to us again.' Ellie told Sylvia about bumping into Tracy outside the *Gazette* offices. 'It doesn't mean that she murdered her husband but it's certainly odd behaviour, isn't it?'

'Yes,' Sylvia agreed. 'In addition to that, Tracy is not *just* an archer. She's better than her ex-husband.' She filled Ellie in on what Nick had told them at the butcher's.

'We need to ask her about it. Shall we pop round? I can pick you up. I'm on my way back to the windmill once I've got petrol.'

'Great. Before you go, Simon rang to say that he and Jen are taking puppy Agatha for her first visit to the groomers and wondered if they could come for supper.'

Simon was Ellie's son and Jen, his girlfriend.

'I tentatively said I thought it would be fine but would check with you and let him know. Shall I make some food? I got some lovely lamb mince from the butcher's earlier. We could have shepherd's pie? He said it would be around 6pm.'

'Lovely. I haven't seen them for a few weeks. I bet the puppy's grown.'

'Finn left a net of cooking apples by the front door. From a tree they cut down. What about apple crumble and custard? I've got a new Nigella recipe that I want to try.'

'Ooh, I'm drooling at the thought. I'll be back soon.' Ellie rang off.

Five minutes later, she was pulling up at one of the pumps on the forecourt of Wootton Garage. As she withdrew the key from the ignition and released her seat belt, she was still turning over the conversation she'd had earlier with Pete at the garden centre.

Why didn't she believe him? It was really bugging her and she couldn't put her finger on what her feeling was based on. She pulled the lever to release the petrol cap and got out.

She was just about to start filling up her car with petrol when she noticed a sign-written pickup truck over at the water and air machine on the garage forecourt. The livery said, 'MORRIS PERSONAL TRAINING' and gave a mobile number. The man who was crouched down beside his front tyre was wearing a baseball cap pulled down over thick, black, wavy hair. Despite his position, it was obvious that he wasn't just tall, he was also heavily built and muscular.

Wasn't that Andy Morris? Tracy's first husband?

Questions rushed into Ellie's mind. She took out her phone and took a quick snap of Andy and his vehicle.

Her instinct was to run over and ask him if they could have a chat, but she sensed she needed to play it cool. She zapped the jeep locks shut, left the pump in its holder, and walked calmly and slowly over to Andy's truck.

His head was down, concentrating on his tyre pressure and moving the heavy rubber flex so that he could reach each of his tyres.

'Hi. Andy? It is Andy, isn't it? You're Liam's dad.'

He looked up, a deep frown crunching his heavy features. 'Yeah. Who are you?'

'I live in Lower Wootton. My name is Ellie Blix.'

'Blix? Your old man's a copper, isn't he?'

Oh God, this was going to be a nightmare.

'What d'you want? I'm in a hurry. I've got to get to work.' He shot her a dirty look, dark eyes unable to conceal his displeasure at being approached.

What was the best angle? Concern for Tracy... or for Liam? She'd have to wing it.

'I'm a friend of Tracy's and Sally's...'

He flinched.

'... and they've asked me to help find out what happened to Robert Seale. I assume you've heard about his death?'

''Course I've heard about it. It's all over the telly and the internet.'

'I have a couple of questions I'd like to ask you, if that's OK?'

'You're not the police. Why should I talk to you?'

'Look, I'm simply trying to help out two friends. Tracy is in trouble.'

He held the air hose still for a moment.

'The police have her down as a suspect, so any information you can give me that helps us to find out what happened will help Tracy.'

He shrugged. Was that a slight softening when she mentioned Tracy?

'She's nothing to do with me. We've been divorced for ages now.'

Ask the questions you want to ask. Don't let him put you off.

'Could you tell me when you last saw Robert, please?'

'I haven't seen him for ages. He's nothing to do with me either. The only person I'm interested in is Liam.' He scowled at her and lifted the rubber hose over the top of her head.

'You didn't see Robert yesterday morning or the night before? At all, anywhere?' Ellie was trying to make sure she covered all bases. Pete had said Andy was at the garden centre by 7.30am and had been walking the dog. That meant he might have been in the woods.

Andy Morris reminded Ellie of a wounded animal. She had no idea what was likely to set him off. The more she could tie his answers down, the better.

He narrowed his eyes. 'Are you for real? I've just told you I haven't seen him for ages. If I'd seen him yesterday morning or the night before, why would I say that?'

Ellie wasn't prepared to be browbeaten. 'I don't know. I'm just trying to be clear about what you're saying. It's very easy to say we haven't seen someone for ages and forget that, actually, we bumped into them in the pub or the supermarket and had forgotten. When did you last speak to him on the phone,' she was babbling, '... or text him, WhatsApp or whatever?'

'I haven't the foggiest. I don't have anything to do with the man. Why on earth would I be chatting to him on the phone? I'm not gonna WhatsApp him photos of my microwave Biryani of an evening, am I?' He snorted.

Ellie groaned inwardly.

'As far as I'm concerned, he nicked my missus and she gave me my marching orders. Now, I might not have been the best husband in the world, but I loved her and didn't want us to split up. I'm certainly not about to have cosy conversations or texting sessions with her new husband.'

'You've made yourself very clear. Thank you. There's just one last question. When did you last see Tracy?'

'I haven't seen her for ages either.'

'Can you remember when that might've been?'

'Actually, yeah, I do remember, now you mention it. The pub. I saw her and that poncey husband of hers in the Windmill three nights ago. Liam and I were in there having a pint and a game of darts and they came in. Ordering Prosecco Bellinis, they were.'

'Did you talk to her?'

'Nah. I've got nothing to say to either of them.' He hung the air hose back up on the machine. 'Is that it? Have I answered all your questions? I've got customers waiting for me at the gym. Can I go and do my job now?'

'Did you not like Tracy's new husband on principle, or was there something specific about him that you didn't like?'

'What do you think? Have you been divorced?'

Ellie felt like saying to him, 'No, but my husband had an affair'.

Instead, she said, 'It's not about what *I* think. This isn't guessing games. Did you, for example, have any run-ins with him?'

'Look. We've had plenty of run-ins over the years – as I'm sure Tracy will be delighted to tell you – but, like I said, nothing recently.'

'You didn't mind Liam living with them?'

'He's hardly ever there. Spends more time at my place or over at Finn Burdett's with Charlie Matthews. That it now?'

'Sorry, I do have one more question actu—'

He groaned loudly. 'How many more *last questions*?'

Ellie ignored him. 'Where were you yesterday morning before you got to the garden centre?'

He gave out a long, slow, gravelly laugh and jangled his keys. Then made towards the driver's door of the pick-up. 'I was wondering when you were going to ask me that one. And, you know what, *Ellie Blix,* I'm not going to answer.'

He gave her a gloating look.

Ellie matched it with a sweet smile. 'Is that because you were in the woods with your dog?'

'Yeah, and I wasn't the only one in the woods, I'll tell you that for free.' With that, he jumped into his cab and slammed the door.

Chapter 17

10am

E llie and Sylvia were in Tracy's lounge. In the fireplace a wood burning stove glowed red, throwing a warm light on the children's toys on the floorboards. In the alcove on one side of the chimney breast a toy-crate was half-full.

'There are a couple of things we are a bit confused about,' Sylvia told Tracy.

She and Ellie took a seat on the sofa.

'What's that?' Tracy replied.

'Why didn't you tell us that you are an excellent archer?'

'Ah.' She blushed. She picked up a plastic doll and a story book and sunk into a chair. 'Sorry about that. With my phone being beside Robert's body, the police got me into a panic. I was scared that you might think I had killed him.'

'Do you still practise?'

'No. It was something Andy and I did together. To be honest, I never enjoyed it. He was very competitive and couldn't stand it when I beat him.'

'Do you still have your archery equipment?'

'No. I gave it away when Andy and I split up.'

Ellie was taking in Tracy's responses. 'You also weren't honest with me about your visit to *The Gazette*,' Ellie said. 'I won't waste time asking you again what Katie Douglas' office is like because I know that you didn't see her. Who did you speak to?'

'Harry Stow.'

'Why did you lie to me?'

Tracy got up and paced across the room. 'I *was* going to see Katie but, on my way through, I passed Harry's office.' She added a couple of logs to the stove. 'You've been there so you know now what the setup is. I've known Harry for years. We used to go to college together. So, when I saw him, I stopped and went into his office to talk to him.'

'Why did you go to see Katie?'

'I went to see her about the article she wrote because I was absolutely furious. But I ended up talking to Harry about it instead because he asked me what I was doing there. I realised that he had known about the article, and he figured out that I was Tracy Seale, the victim's wife.'

'What did you want Katie to do?'

'It was some of the stuff that you were talking about. I wanted her to understand that, in publishing all of that sensitive information the police had not yet revealed, she could have compromised the investigation. I told Harry all of this, and quickly realised I was wasting my time. At college he was all over the ethics of reporting but when I spoke to him, it was obvious that this isn't something that he cares about at all anymore.' She paused. 'You've seen that new building. You commented on it. I have no idea where he's getting his money from, but I strongly suspect that not all of it is legal.' She sighed deeply. 'I'm sorry. I should have been straight with you.'

'Yes, you should have. You asked us to investigate your husband's murder. Is there anything else that you haven't been honest with us about?'

She shook her head. 'Sorry.'

'Just in case, can you confirm whether there are any other people that Robert had fallen out with?'

They were still talking when there was a knock at the front door.

Tracy jumped. 'Who on earth is that? Scared the life out of me.'

Ellie stood up. 'I'll go. You stay there. It's probably just someone coming round to offer their condolences.' She walked down the hall to the door and opened it.

Standing in front of her was a young woman in a long, red parka. She had a sour expression, deep brown hair and was holding the hand of a little girl who must have been about four years old. The girl was clutching a fluffy teddy in her arms and holding flowers.

'Are you Tracy Seale?' There was something about her tone which alarmed Ellie. It was accusatory and entitled.

'I'm not, no. I'm a friend of hers. You are?'

'I'm Rob Seale's wife.' A shadow seemed to pass over her and she fixed a steely gaze on Ellie.

She hadn't given her first name. She had simply referred to herself as 'Rob Seale's wife'. And '*Rob*'? Tracy called him 'Robert'.

Ellie tried to process the news, to make sense of what the woman had just said. Perhaps Tracy and Robert weren't married?

'Hang on a minute. I'll get Tracy. This is going to be a shock for her.'

'Who is it?' Tracy must have heard voices and was striding towards Ellie now.

'This lady says that she is—'

'*Rob's wife*,' the woman repeated.

125

Tracy edged closer, frowning in confusion.

Ellie stepped aside to allow her to move into the doorway.

'Do you mean Robert? You can't be. *I am* Robert's wife.'

'I can assure you I am. My name is Chrissy Seale.' There was an unmistakeable look of challenge in her eyes.

'W... what is she talking about?' Tracy stared at Ellie and then turned back to the woman. 'Who are you?'

Chrissy's manner was impatient. 'Robert and I have been married for the last five years. The first I heard about you was from the police when they came round to tell me about his death.' She paused briefly to take a breath. 'Presumably you're divorced?'

Tracy was holding onto the door handle, her face as white as paper.

Ellie got the impression she hadn't heard Chrissy's question.

Chrissy extracted an envelope from her bag and continued. 'I've brought his will. Just so that there's no confusion about where we all stand in terms of his estate. My solicitor has the original document.' The woman was still standing on the doorstep, clutching the hand of the little girl.

Tracy seemed to notice the child. 'Who's this?'

The little girl rocked her teddy and gave it a kiss. In one hand she held bluebells.

'This is Poppy. Our daughter.' The woman stared at Tracy, looking mutinous.

Ellie studied the little girl.

She was definitely Robert's child. She had his large brown eyes and high forehead. His wavy brown hair.

Chrissy waved the envelope in Tracy's direction. 'This copy is for you.'

Tracy's face drained of colour. She extended her hand to take the envelope, stumbled and reached for the door frame. 'Sorry... I'm finding it... hard to take in... what you're saying. Did you say that you and Robert have been married for five years?'

'That's correct.' She flapped the envelope at Tracy. 'We live just outside Canterbury. Got married at a little church in one of the villages. Harbledown.'

'I... If what you're saying is true—'

'It *is* true.'

'If what you're saying is true, that means that Robert got married to you while he was married to me. He and I are *still* married.'

'You what? You're not divorced?' Her face clouded over, as though questions were crowding in. 'Are you sure?' Chrissy tutted loudly, as if Tracy had made a mistake.

'Of course I'm sure.'

'Why would he have married me if he was still married to you? It doesn't make sense.'

'Tracy, do you want to invite the lady in?' Ellie said softly. 'It's not the easiest topic to discuss on the doorstep.'

'I'm sorry. I can't... I just can't... How can he have...?' Tracy was babbling. Her gaze flitted about as if she was looking for answers.

Chrissy leaned round her and chucked the envelope on the hall table. 'Anyway – I'll leave this with you.' And, with that, she wheeled round and marched back down the path with Poppy in tow.

Tracy stood watching. When Chrissy disappeared from view, Tracy dropped to the floor like a collapsed umbrella.

Chapter 18

11.15am

It was after eleven by the time Ellie and Sylvia had settled Tracy following Chrissy's bombshell and made sure she was OK. The news had blown things wide open.

As soon as they were out of Tracy's earshot, Sylvia said, 'One of my colleagues dealt with a case of bigamy. I'm pretty sure it renders the second marriage void.'

They were walking away from the house towards the jeep.

Ellie shook her head. This was what she was worried about. 'If that's the case, Chrissy might not have any legal protection at all. It's going to be a nightmare for both of them.'

The two women went their separate ways. Sylvia wanted to walk through the village to pick up some baking ingredients and get a loaf from the baker's. Ellie continued walking back to the jeep.

With Tracy's permission, she had photographed the address listed on the will for Chrissy and Poppy. The police were already in touch with Chrissy, she had said, so they wouldn't be interfering by going over there to talk further with her about Robert.

Both women had to be going through hell.

They had not just grief to deal with now but also the betrayal of the person who had just died. And for Chrissy, a legally non-existent marriage.

Thank goodness Tracy had her sister, Sally, and Liam. They hadn't had the opportunity to find out from Chrissy who she had for support.

Ellie would have to wait to find out from Sylvia what light her social work training could shed on it all.

She zapped the jeep's locks open, got in and checked her messages.

There was a text from Zoe, asking where she was.

And a WhatsApp from a cleaning customer, giving two weeks' notice to cancel their contract.

'Oh crikey,' she said aloud. 'Not another one.'

The Langs hadn't been customers of Ellie's for very long, but they had four holiday homes which she cleaned regularly.

Together with the call centre from earlier in the week and Gladys Blackman, this was the third cancellation in a few days.

Ellie couldn't decide the best way to handle the situation. The last thing she wanted was to be aggressive and start tarnishing a fifteen-year reputation.

Perhaps she was lucky nothing like this had happened before. Only on one occasion when a couple of sixth form students had finished their spring exams and were waiting to go to university. They had decided it would be fun to offer cleaning services in the village, printed out leaflets on their parents' old inkjet printer and stuffed them through letterboxes. However, when it came to *actually doing the work*, they soon discovered that running a cleaning business was not quite the 'fun' they had envisaged. Having left one property unlocked, caused a flood in another and lost the pet rabbit in a third, they had to admit they'd made a mistake.

This new situation, however, was much more perplexing.

Ellie knew there was nothing wrong with the standard of Blix Blitz cleaning, and she also knew that, on the rare occasions when one of her staff made a mistake or broke something, they always told her, and she informed the customer. Therefore, it seemed unlikely that people were cancelling their contracts because they were unhappy with the service she was providing.

Nor did this sound like a bunch of teenagers.

It sounded much more organised and systematic.

When she got home, she would chase up the enquiries that she and Zoe had made about other cleaning companies in the area. She would ring the Langs and find out why they wanted to cancel. That would give her time to think about what she wanted to say, and to chat it through with Sylvia.

But there was no escaping it.

Ellie *had* to stop the cascade of customer cancellations before it finished her business. Having scraped through exceptionally difficult times before Christmas, she did not want to go back to struggling again.

She sent Zoe a quick text, saying she would be back at the windmill shortly and that Sylvia had gone to get some food.

Her stomach lurched when she saw a voicemail from Dave. Her body was racked with tension as she prepared to listen.

'Hey Ells. Quick call before I go into morning briefing.'

His voice.

'Just wanted to say that, although it ended prematurely, it was lovely spending time with you last night. I'm really sorry

about Ruby's text message. Obviously, I'm not responsible for her actions but nevertheless I'm sad that our evening together ended early because of them. I'm not going to repeat all the other stuff I said, except to say that I love you and my life is not complete without you.'

Ellie released a huge sigh.

Was that what she had been expecting?

In her mind, she sifted through the last eighteen months. The stakes had been so high, she had been scared of the worst and hadn't allowed herself to hope for the best.

She hadn't slept particularly well, and had, of course, dreamt about Dave on and off. She hadn't met Ruby in person – had she? – so she had no idea what she looked like. But in Ellie's dream, 'Ruby' had long black hair and dark brown eyes. In the dream, Ellie had called round to Dave's flat and the two of them had been there on the sofa together, watching a film. Ruby was in a dressing gown and had her hair tied up with a scrunchie that Dave had told her was Zoe's.

Ellie knew dreams weren't reality, and this was her unconscious mind's way of playing tricks on her, of shoving in her face all the things that she was scared of.

Nevertheless, part of Ellie had wondered whether there was more to come from Ruby and whether Dave's proclamations were too good to be true.

She replayed his voicemail.

I love you and my life is not complete without you.

Perhaps they weren't too good to be true.

A huge grin spread over her face.

'He loves me,' she said. 'And I love him. So, *you*, Ruby CSI, can flipping well leave us alone.'

Dave wasn't a weak man. She had never believed that people were lured into affairs against their will. For Dave to have begun a relationship with Andrea, there had to have been a part of him that had wanted it, however briefly. And although this still hurt, she also knew Dave was not going to have a fling or start a relationship with Ruby unless he wanted to.

And now, everything he said indicated that he *didn't*.

Perhaps there was a way for them after all?

Should she reply to Dave's message? She didn't want to ring in case he answered. She could send him a quick text.

Except she didn't have anything to say.

Ellie decided to leave it, to get on with her day and allow her feelings to settle. She checked her watch, opened the Blix Blitz diary and scanned for any changes. She and Zoe were down to do an Airbnb changeover in the village at 2pm.

Her stomach rumbled loudly, and she realised she hadn't eaten since breakfast. The Airbnb changeover at this property always involved a lot of heavy lifting and ironing, both things which Ellie found tiring. She would nip home and grab a quick sandwich, pick up Zoe and they could head off to the job together.

Tracy's house was very close to the windmill and Ellie had a sudden yearning to see the sea. She put the jeep into gear and drove off, immediately turning left onto the road which ran along the sea front.

On her right, the large, detached houses looked splendid in the spring sunshine. It was the style on this stretch of the road for the properties to have glorious wrought iron verandas running along the front on the first floor. Looking at these briefly as she passed them made Ellie smile. She adored living in the old, converted windmill, and couldn't envisage living anywhere else, but, on occasions, she wondered what it would be like to own one of these grand buildings, with their beautiful, pointed roofs and turrets, overlooking the sea. She imagined herself getting up in the morning and taking her tea over to the window with Rebus and enjoying the view. She knew, from cleaning in them, that they had large rooms with high ceilings and beautiful cornices and fireplaces.

Once she had passed the houses, her thoughts drifted to Robert's murder.

To all the things that she had learned from Tracy, and Sally, and Pete.

And now there was Chrissy's information to factor into their calculations. A multitude of questions began circulating. What was going on with Pete? She really needed to discuss it with Sylvia and Zoe, and talk to Sally again. Then there was Tracy's ex-husband, Andy Morris. Had he been deliberately messing around with his parting comment, or might he be a suspect?

Perhaps, if Sylvia was back home, they'd have the opportunity to assess where they were before Ellie and Zoe headed out.

Leaving the coast road now, Ellie turned right and headed back towards home. In the distance, the windmill rose tall. The earlier drizzle had passed and the white sails shone in the sunlight. She drove around the village green. Alan, who ran the village bistro, was throwing a ball for his spaniel, Lily. On the pond, ducks were merrily swimming along with their chicks.

She beeped the car horn at Bob and Finn, who were busy erecting the sheep pen for the Open Day.

Outside the Windmill Inn, the car park was packed with Range Rovers, BMWs and sports cars.

Just as Ellie was about to turn into her drive, she saw a woman near the front door of the windmill.

What was she doing?

It looked like she was searching for something around the flowerpots by the front door. Who the hell was it?

Instinct kicked in and Ellie rammed her hand on the car horn.

The woman jumped and stumbled, quickly regaining her balance and shooting a dirty look in Ellie's direction.

Ellie flung open the car door and got out. 'Can I help you?'

'Oh. I... I was just—'

'... looking for something?' Ellie strode towards her, furious. 'This is my house. Who are you and what are you doing here?'

A peculiar feeling crept over Ellie. It was the long black hair and dark brown eyes. The slim build. The woman was wearing jeans, a cotton type shirt with a black leather jacket on top.

Very similar to Ellie's dream, when a woman had been on the sofa in Dave's flat.

'I recognise you. You're Ruby, aren't you? The CSI that works with Dave. You sent me that horrible text message last night.'

She looked so similar to Ellie's dream that they must have met before in real life. Where had that been?

The woman didn't answer.

'What are you looking for around my pots?'

It was where they usually kept their spare front door key, but Ellie had moved it after the burglary at the Matthews' house.

The woman froze for a couple of moments then leapt away from the door.

'Did you hear me? What are you looking for?'

Surely though, this woman, if she was Ruby, Dave's CSI colleague at work, she wouldn't turn up at Ellie's house and let herself in, would she?

'Nothing. I'm not looking for anything.'

'What are you doing here then?'

'Nothing.'

'Don't say "nothing". That's ridiculous. You obviously came here for a reason. What was it?'

'It doesn't matter now.'

'It does. I don't want you coming here. First, you send me a horrible text message, telling me lies to deliberately upset and hurt me. Then you show up at my house.' Ellie walked towards her. She had no idea what she was going to do or say but she couldn't control the ball of anger that was growing within her.

Ruby flashed Ellie a look of indignation. 'You think they were lies, do you?' She gave a hollow, sneering laugh and her expression changed. No longer indignation, now it was temper. 'You obviously don't know Dave as well as you think you do.'

'I've known him since we were small kids. Literally. We've grown up together. We went to all the same schools, the same sixth form college. Now, everyone round here knows he had an affair. Katie Douglas mentioned it in the local paper when Andrea Burdett was murdered before Christmas. But he has assured me that the things you wrote in your text message last night are categorically not true. And I believe him.'

'You would, wouldn't you? But he's not telling you the truth because he doesn't want to hurt you.'

'I'm sorry, I just don't believe you. If it's over between us, why has he just told me that he loves me and that his life isn't complete without me?'

'Because he feels sorry for you.'

Ouch.

'Anyway, I'll leave you to your *sad delusions*.' Ruby emphasised the last two words. 'I've got things to do. It's our day off. We're going to the Windmill Inn for coffee if you'd like to tag along?'

'It might be your day off but Dave's at work,' Ellie told her.

'Is he?' She gave Ellie a knowing smile.

'We've met before, haven't we? Where?'

'Don't you remember?' Ruby moved towards her. 'Well, I'm not telling you.'

And, with that, she flounced off down the drive and onto Pennypot Lane.

For a few moments, Ellie stood frozen to the spot.

What on earth had just happened?

She couldn't believe the cheek of Ruby, turning up like this after telling Dave that she would leave Ellie alone.

And being so aggressive and provocative.

Ellie grabbed her bag from the jeep and watched Ruby's rear view disappear into the pub next door. Ellie wanted to make sure the woman had gone before she went inside her home.

Ruby had clearly decided she wanted Dave and she was going to make sure she got him, regardless of who she hurt.

Ellie suspected she was not done with her antics.

There were other concerns forming in Ellie's mind, however, and she wasn't sure which possibility bothered her most. Ruby either hadn't been honest with Dave last night, or she'd changed her mind this morning.

Or Dave was lying.

Chapter 19

12.15pm

The ground floor of the windmill had a solid brick construction, which was tar-painted on the outside. The inside was a combination of exposed brickwork and white, painted plaster – with a network of horizontal and vertical beams.

When Ellie came in, Sylvia was up a decorator's ladder. She had fetched her duster-on-a-stick from her own house and was going over the windmill's timber beams. *The Archers* was on full blast on Radio 4. Since Zoe had shown Sylvia how to use the app, she was enjoying catching up on missed episodes.

'She refuses to come down and let me do it,' Zoe shouted over the radio drama, her foot on the bottom rung of the ladder to stop it from slipping.

'I'm fine,' Sylvia shouted back. 'I'm sixty-five not ninety-five. And don't talk about me like I'm not here.' She reached for another giant piece of timber and flicked the feather duster with even greater determination.

Ellie coughed and darted out of the way of the dust cloud, dabbing at her nose. 'I am concerned about you falling.' She sneezed. 'Also – are you sure the vacuum wouldn't be better? I only hoovered down here yest– Oh, for the love of God, can someone turn that noise down?'

Sylvia didn't answer. Ellie might run a cleaning company, but it didn't mean she knew everything. Sometimes the old ways were best.

Ellie switched the speakers off at the mains and silence descended on the room.

'I can see where Dad gets his stubbornness from now,' Zoe said, chuckling. 'And, yes, Gran,' she said, raising her voice, I did mean you to hear that.'

'Could you please *stop* teaching your grandmother how to use technology?' Ellie asked Zoe. 'If I have to listen to one more episode of *The Archers*, I shall not be responsible for my actions.'

Although she spoke loudly, Sylvia caught a weariness in Ellie's voice.

'I think I'll tuck into some of the cakes for the open day,' Ellie said from the kitchen.

Sylvia gripped the ladder and glanced down at the worktop. Ellie was deliberately opening all the tins and containers, knowing it would get Sylvia down off the ladder. 'Don't do that,' she snapped. 'You'll let air in.'

'I think you mean *dust*?' Zoe said.

Ellie started telling them about Ruby turning up. They hadn't heard the commotion due to the radio volume.

'I got home about fifteen minutes before you,' Sylvia said. 'Ruby wasn't here then. Unless she was hiding in the bushes – or her car – I would have seen her, surely?'

'Cheeky cow,' Zoe said. 'Are you going to tell Dad that she was here?' she asked her mum.

'Yes. He needs to know what she's up to.'

Sylvia clambered back down the steps, cheeks flushed. 'I feel like ringing him and telling him now.' When Dave had admitted to his affair, she'd tried not to take sides, but in the eighteen months since, it hadn't been easy. Dave's betrayal had caused Ellie immense pain. She could see they both wanted to get back together, but she also knew Ellie was terrified of him hurting her again, and this Ruby woman needed sorting out.

'Please don't,' Ellie replied. She told Zoe about Ruby's text message in the woods the evening before.

'The woman's obsessed. This is turning into stalking.' Now that Sylvia was off the ladder, Zoe joined her mother over at the worktop by the sink.

Fifteen minutes later, Ellie, Sylvia and Zoe were sitting at the kitchen table. Sylvia had bought a sourdough loaf from the baker's and had made sandwiches for the three of them.

Ellie told them Ruby had hinted she was meeting Dave for coffee.

'In the pub next door?' Zoe asked through a mouthful of smoked ham, mozzarella and basil.' She slapped her lunch down on the plate. 'Right. There's only one way to find out if that's true.' She got up and marched towards the front door.

'We can't spy on them,' Ellie said. 'I refuse to sink that low. If they are meeting for lunch, let them get on with it. She's not going to endear herself to anyone if she's lying, is she?'

Zoe grabbed her jacket and pulled it on. 'No, Mum. You don't have to come with me but *I* want to know what he's up to.' She swept out of the house, letting the door slam.

Ellie plonked her sandwich down on the plate in front of her. She sat still for a few moments. 'Let's keep talking, shall we, so I don't have to imagine the scenes next door.'

Sylvia obliged. 'What's your gut feeling about what Ruby was doing here?' She fiddled with the salad on her plate. 'Do you really think she was looking for the door key?'

'I think it's unlikely. She must've known someone could be in?'

'Would've thought so. And she's a CSI. I'm pretty sure she'd lose her job if she was found guilty of letting herself into a property for personal reasons.'

'Definitely. But if that's what she was planning, it's a bit unhinged.' Ellie narrowed her eyes as though she was running the scene through in her mind. 'She was moving the pots and peering round each one. I'm sure she was looking for something.'

'How would she know that's where we used to keep the key? I'm sure lots of people in the village do, but only friends and people who come here regularly.'

Ellie shivered. 'Ugh. I hope she hasn't been watching the house.'

Sylvia stabbed a piece of tomato with her fork. She was tempted to speak to Ruby's line manager.

'I don't even want to think about it. The other option is that she wanted to speak to me, but in that case, surely she would have knocked at the door?'

'Perhaps she was intending to knock and lost her nerve?' Sylvia suggested, although it didn't seem likely.

'Her manner didn't lack confidence though.' Ellie picked at the salad on her plate. 'The other thing that was disconcerting is that I'm pretty sure I've met her somewhere.' Ellie told Sylvia that Ruby had looked similar to the woman in her dream. 'Thing is, I can't for the life of me figure out when – or where?'

'Dave might know.'

'Yes, I'll probably ask him when I speak to him about it.' She paused. 'I'm building up to that.'

The front door opened.

Rebus barked and zoomed off to greet Zoe, who came bowling in.

'No sign of Dad.' Zoe was slightly out of breath. 'Either Ruby was telling porkies or he blew her out.'

'She was lying,' Sylvia stated emphatically.

'She's there on her own.' Zoe hung her jacket up and came back over to the table. 'Eating cheesecake and playing with her phone.'

'Did you speak to her?' Ellie asked. 'Please tell me that you didn't have a go at her?'

'No, I didn't speak to her. And I didn't go out of my way to make sure that she saw me or didn't see me.' Zoe took a bite from her sandwich and seemed to be studying the filling intently. 'I wasn't prepared to hide behind pillars and all that rubbish. If she complains to Dad about me spying on her, I'll tell him the truth. I went to see if he was there.' She turned and faced her mother and grandmother defiantly. 'Anyway – what were you talking about? Have I missed anything critical?'

'No, but there *is* something you don't know about,' Ellie replied. She told Zoe about Chrissy Seale.

'*Bigamy?* You're kidding?' Her hand jerked and a lump of mozzarella fell off her sandwich and onto the floor.

'*Zoe.*' Sylvia didn't intend her tone to be so teacher-y.

Rebus arrived in a flash and hoovered up the cheesy morsel straight away.

'Never mind,' Zoe told Sylvia. 'Didn't go to waste.'

Ellie groaned. 'It's like having young children all over again.' She checked the time on the kitchen clock. 'We've got just over an hour before Zoe and I need to be at our next appointment. Shall we take stock of where we are with Robert's murder?'

Chapter 20

12.45pm

'Have the police released any updates?' Ellie was sitting round the kitchen table with Sylvia and Zoe, discussing Robert's murder. 'I know they're always cautious about what they make, but I haven't heard of any developments, have you?'

Sylvia replied immediately. 'Just continued appeals in the media for witnesses.'

'Same as Gran,' Zoe said. 'I've got Google alerts set. Nada.'

'OK,' Ellie said. 'Given we've started discussing them, let's kick off with Robert Seale's other wife and family. How does this change what we know?'

'It's got to complicate Robert's murder, surely?' Zoe replied. 'We've been thinking about Tracy, Pete and Andy.

Now we need to consider Nick too, and people related to Chrissy and Robert's relationship—'

'Who we might not know,' Sylvia added. 'There are now more people who could potentially feel aggrieved with Robert. It's going to make our job harder.'

'As well as finding out who's poaching our cleaning clients,' Ellie said.

'It's one thing for Chrissy to turn up saying, "Hello, I am the new wife".' Sylvia cut up an apple. 'It's completely different to turn up with his *will*.'

'She meant business, didn't she?' Ellie said. 'I wonder if she knows that the second wife effectively has no rights?'

'Hmm. Who else might have known that Robert had two "wives" – apart from Robert himself?' Zoe asked.

'That's the sixty-million-dollar question, isn't it?' Sylvia said. 'Did you notice that Tracy and Chrissy were both insistent that they did *not* know about each other?'

'Did you get the impression they were both telling the truth?' Zoe asked.

'It was hard to tell,' said Ellie. 'Tracy fainted, so unless she's a good actress it must've been a shock.'

'I doubt Tracy knew. But it's harder to gauge with Chrissy. Partly because she delivered her news and scarpered. Also, because she knew what she was coming to say. So, if she knew about Tracy, she would've had time to practise her act.'

'If she knew he'd been married, might that have given her motivation to get rid of him?' Zoe asked. 'I haven't a clue how the law works with bigamy. I hadn't even heard of a real-life case of it until today.'

'From what I can remember, it's the person who is already married who's in trouble. I guess if you find out your new spouse has an existing one, and you bump them off, you get rid of the evidence. You reduce the risk of people finding out and it being splashed all over the newspapers—'

'... and the internet... *forever*.' Zoe pinched a quarter of Sylvia's apple. She was shaking her head. 'I'm sorry but these are sleepy Kent villages. I can't get my head round the idea of bigamy.'

Ellie told Zoe about the wedding in Harbledown. 'It'd be interesting to know who was there.'

'We've got her address,' said Sylvia, 'Dave said I can use his car again, so I thought I'd pop over there after lunch.'

Ellie and Zoe caught each other's eye. Dave was notoriously protective of his Audi.

'I hope you feel privileged,' Zoe said. 'I left chewing gum in the ashtray, and I'm banned from driving it forever.'

'That's gross,' said Sylvia, pulling a disgusted face. 'I'd ban you for that too.'

'Good idea about visiting Chrissy,' said Ellie. 'If you have time, perhaps you could visit the vicar on the way back? Find out who attended. See who was their best man and woman.'

'Will do.'

'I'll have a dig around online,' Zoe said. 'See what I can find out about Chrissy. If she didn't know he was married, she'll have shared wedding and family photos.'

'That must've been tricky,' Ellie said. 'Surely Robert wouldn't have wanted her splashing wedding pictures on the internet?'

'I'll get on it and report back.'

Ellie glanced at the clock on the kitchen wall. 'Changing the subject... I bumped into Andy Morris earlier, Tracy's ex-husband.' She told Zoe and Sylvia what Andy had said to her.

'So, he was in the woods before he went to the garden centre,' Sylvia said, 'and saw someone else there, but wouldn't say who?'

'We need to find out who that person was.' Zoe was tapping on the table impatiently. 'If only we had access to CCTV, like Dad does. Either of them could have had the opportunity to kill Robert.'

'We know Andy is a skilled archer,' Ellie added.

'He's got a rescue greyhound,' Zoe said. 'Finn told me. He takes her into Appledown Woods really early so he can let her off the lead.'

'One of us can check with Andy. He works at the gym.' Ellie knew where it was.

'I'll go,' said Sylvia. 'I'm used to people like him. We can have a chat about his dog.'

Ellie swiped her phone screen and brought up the photograph she had snapped of Andy at the garage. 'This is him. I've met him before in the pub with Finn and Zoe. Liam and Finn are mates. Liam brought his dad over to join us for a drink and we got stuck with him for about an hour. It was excruciating.'

'Why was that?'

'All he did was slag everyone off. He seems to be permanently angry.'

'Sounds a charmer,' Sylvia replied. 'Didn't Liam mind?'

'Liam seems to hero worship him. I'm not sure he noticed, or minded, if he did. Maybe he ignores it out of loyalty.' Ellie paused to think. 'I would have thought it would be worth sounding Liam out. He might know what his dad was up to. Why was he at the garden centre so early? He might be able to give us a bit more background on Robert too.'

'Finn and I are meeting Charlie and Liam later,' Zoe said. 'If we get the chance, we'll ask Liam.'

'Great,' Ellie replied. 'Thanks. I've also been thinking that it would be useful to ask Nick Matthews if he has any more of the arrows like the ones that they had stolen.'

'We can ask Charlie if he could grab one from home and bring it round.' Zoe was making notes in her phone. 'Or WhatsApp us a picture.'

Ellie was still pondering. 'It seems like there are either a lot of coincidences in this case – or whoever is responsible has gone to a lot of trouble to plan and carry out preparation.'

Zoe and Sylvia were nodding.

'For example, if the arrow that killed Robert was one of those stolen from the Matthews' house, it suggests that the burglary was carried out strategically.'

'And assuming that Tracy was telling us the truth about her phone,' Sylvia added, 'somebody went to the trouble of stealing it in order to be able to plant it next to the body.' She sucked in a breath. 'The thing is, that's *not* impulse killing. That's *not* someone who snapped in the moment. It's someone who's put a lot of thought into what they're going to do, how they're going to do it and when, and what they need. Don't you think?'

'I agree entirely,' Ellie said. 'Let's consider everyone in terms of means, motive and opportunity. What about Nick Matthews?' She pulled a face, feeling uncomfortable talking this way about their friends and neighbours.

None of them spoke.

They just stared at each other.

'It's really hard, isn't it?' Sylvia said.

'These are our friends,' Ellie added.

'On my social work training, we were always taught that it was important to consider whether a particular action was within a person's behavioural repertoire. In other words, Nick and Pete may have been furious with Robert, but do we really think they are killers?'

'Isn't that the point though?' Zoe answered. 'Lots of people could *potentially* kill if they were pushed. But what does a killer look like? Nick and Pete don't *look like* killers because we can't imagine them killing. That's because we know and like them.'

'All we can do really is consider each aspect as clinically as we can,' Ellie suggested. 'There is no doubt that both Nick and Pete were furious with Robert over his behaviour at the farm shop. He caused them both considerable grief and cost them a lot of money. Would they gain from killing him? If they wanted revenge, yes. But killing him isn't going to help them get back the money that he owes them.'

'The other thing we were taught on our training is that when people commit crimes, their thinking has a logic to it. It might not seem rational from the outside, but, inside their head, it makes sense. The crime that they carry out is effective. It serves its purpose,' said Sylvia.

'Finn and I watch loads of those true crime shows and they always talk about that, don't they?' Zoe added. 'That it's pointless to look for motives that might look logical to the outsider. It's about getting inside the heads of each person and understanding the specific circumstances of their lives.'

'*And* their personalities,' Sylvia added.

'I think that means we can't afford to lump Pete and Nick into one category,' said Ellie. 'They are different people and might *not* have been affected to the same extent, and in the same way, by Robert's actions.'

'Well, Nick obviously has the archery expertise.' Sylvia was counting out the factors on her fingers. 'He had a grievance with Robert. Did he have the opportunity to go and kill him at 5am? We don't know yet.'

'Like Nick, Pete had a beef with Robert. He's got some archery experience. We need to find out where he was first thing yesterday. What about Andy Morris?'

'In terms of capability, he comes across as a bully. It would be easy to underestimate him, but I suspect that underneath all that, he's pretty sharp.'

'He *definitely* is intelligent,' Zoe replied. 'We were in a quiz team with him in the pub one night. He's got a degree in sports psychology.'

'Wow. I would not have expected that.'

'I've just realised that I haven't relayed what Pete told me when I went up to the garden centre.' Ellie filled Sylvia and Zoe in on the key points.

The flood.

Nick helping Pete before and after the wedding.

'When he was talking to me,' Ellie told them, 'I kept getting the feeling that something wasn't right. Either that he wasn't telling me the truth or that there was something that he *wasn't* telling me. I couldn't put my finger on it. And it really bothers me because I've known him as long as I've known Dave and Sally.'

'That's where I think this behavioural repertoire thing is useful,' Sylvia said. 'Under normal circumstances we would all say that of course Pete and Nick couldn't kill anyone. But when we sense that's something odd is going on, or something additional, or something we don't know about, it makes us wonder whether it could be possible.'

'I can see what you mean,' Ellie said.

'I had a client once whose partner seemed as nice as pie,' Sylvia explained. 'One day, he flipped, and his behaviour only made sense when we found out that there had been something in the background triggering him. In this instance, it was childhood trauma. Initially, none of us would have thought he was capable of violence, and it wasn't until we understood his background, that it made sense.'

'The Pete situation is tricky because he's Sally's partner. Have you talked to her about him yet, Mum?'

'Not yet. And I feel bad about that. She's my best friend. I haven't said anything to her, partly because I know that she's worried about his behaviour, and I am too.'

'You're just going to have to tell her exactly that, then, aren't you?' Sylvia chipped in with her usual pragmatism. 'Maybe see if you can put your finger on what it was that unsettled you, and then simply be honest with her.'

'Thing is, Mum, she and Tracy have asked us to investigate Robert's murder so we're going to have to tell them the truth. I don't think that Sally is going to think badly of you for being honest with her about what Pete has told you. She trusts you. That's why she's asked us to help,' said Zoe. 'Everyone trusts you. It's why they all open up to you and tell you their secrets.'

'I agree,' said Sylvia. 'You might find that when you talk to Sally, the two of you can figure out what it is that feels off. And, God forbid, if Pete was involved with some aspect of Robert's death, she's going to want to know. She has a right to know.'

'Gran's right.'

'I'll have a mull, see if I can pin down what's bothering me, and have a chat with Sal. Thanks, you two.' Ellie paused. The other thing she wanted to discuss was Tracy. 'Can we talk about Tracy's phone? What do we think about her explanation? Is it possible that she *could* have been in the woods herself and dropped it?'

'Do you mean, did she kill Robert?' Sylvia asked.

'Well, that too, I suppose. We know she's a skilled archer.' Ellie looked at Zoe. 'I was more thinking along the lines of, at the most benign, might she have been in the woods and seen Robert's body? Dropped her phone while she was there? And, less benign, she could, I suppose, have been a helper or a spectator. I'm just thinking aloud really. Any thoughts?'

'What would Tracy gain from getting rid of Robert?' Sylvia asked. 'She told us that she had wanted to divorce him but agreed to give him another chance. So, although she could have got rid of him legally, maybe she wasn't up to the series of confrontations and conflict that divorce would have created? There has to be a sort of consent, or acceptance, to it.'

'Gran, you're a genius. Murdering someone gets rid of the need for all that.' Zoe's face was full of excitement. 'They show this in those true crime programmes too. People don't *agree* to be killed. It's something one person *imposes* on another.'

'In other words, people often resort to murder when they've tried other things to achieve whatever it is that they want and have failed,' Ellie suggested. 'Put like that, it means that almost anyone could be capable of murder.'

'Yes,' Sylvia said. 'That's what I've always believed.'

'You're amazing, Gran.' Zoe laughed. She stacked up their plates and loaded them in the dishwasher.

'Right,' Sylvia added. 'I need to get a wriggle on. Collect Chrissy and see if I can get her and Tracy talking.'

Chapter 21

1.50pm

Zoe reached the jeep before Ellie and pointed at the plain white postcard under the windscreen wiper. 'What's that?'

They were on their way to their cleaning job.

'Hopefully it's a flyer for that flipping new cleaning company. Grab it up, lovey, will you? At least we'll know what they say now.'

Zoe lifted the wiper and extracted the card. She read the text. 'You'd better call Dad.' She snapped a pic of the message with her phone and passed the card to her mum. 'It's a death threat.'

On one side, it said, 'Ellie Blix'.

On the other side, there was a message. Ellie read the words, barely able to take them in.

'*You need to learn when to quit. It would be awful if you ended up like Robert Seale.*'

A wave of nausea swept over Ellie and her legs went weak. She grabbed Zoe's arm. 'That's horrible.' Shaking, she teased one of Rebus' poo bags out of her pocket and stuffed it at Zoe. 'There might be prints on it.' Her voice was barely audible. 'Stick it in this.'

It would be awful if you ended up like Robert Seale.

Ellie leant against the car and dialled Dave's mobile number.

Chapter 22

2pm

T racy's kitchen was at the rear of the house, with French windows looking onto a small walled garden.

Sylvia had collected Robert's second wife, Chrissy, from Canterbury and brought her back to Tracy's house. She was with Chrissy and her daughter, Poppy, in the kitchen because Tracy had shut herself in the lounge and was refusing to speak to anyone. They were waiting for Liam to arrive and help mediate.

'You must have had a dreadful shock when the police told you about Tracy.' Sylvia was trying to put herself in Chrissy's shoes and see if she had any idea about Robert's other family. It was easy to feel angry with her for turning up at Tracy's door and ambushing her, but if she genuinely hadn't known anything about Robert's other family, Sylvia didn't blame her for wanting some answers. She had been a bit aggressive when she arrived at the door, but maybe she'd been suffering from the same sort of shock and disbelief as Tracy, and had wanted to confirm that Tracy and Robert were divorced.

'That's putting it mildly,' Chrissy replied. 'I was hoping I could leave Poppy with the neighbours, but they were out so I had to bring her.'

'Mummy, where's Daddy? Is he coming home soon?' Poppy was wearing a floral dress over black leggings, with a pretty cardigan over the top. She had brought her teddy with her again.

'I've tried to explain,' Chrissy whispered to Sylvia, 'but I don't think she understood.'

Sylvia caught the expression on the young woman's face. From her own children, she knew how easy it was to assume that because they'd heard everything, they understood everything. It was hard not to feel angry with a man who had deceived two women and created families with both.

'I'm not sure yet, sweetheart. Mummy needs to talk to these nice ladies first and find out what's happened.' Chrissy paused and closed her eyes for a few moments.

Sylvia wondered how she was going to explain to Poppy that her father was dead. It was obvious the little girl adored her dad.

'Daddy is at the hospital. He's been in an accident and, unfortunately, he's not coming back to us. He was very badly hurt, and the angels have taken him to heaven.'

'But how can he be in heaven if he's at the hospital?'

Sylvia held her breath.

Poppy came and climbed up on her mum's lap, sitting sideways so that she could look at her face. She kicked her legs and a squashed bluebell fell off the tread of Chrissy's boot.

'Well, his body is in a special place at the hospital. It's where people go when they've died. And Daddy *has* died, sweetheart. Like Matilda died. Do you remember?' She whispered to Sylvia, 'Matilda was Poppy's hamster.'

'Daddy gave me Tilda,' Poppy explained to Sylvia earnestly. 'We've got a Labbidor now,' she stumbled over the word, 'called Coco.'

'That's lovely,' Sylvia replied. 'I like dogs. We've got one too.'

Chrissy stroked her daughter's hair, tucking a wayward strand behind her ear. 'So, Daddy's body is at the hospital, but his spirit may have left and gone to heaven. Do you remember, like with Matilda, when we buried her in the garden, we did a little ceremony and wished her well on her journey to heaven?'

'Is Daddy with Matilda then?'

'I don't know. He might be. Would you like that? Would you like Daddy and Matilda to be together in heaven, with Grandma?'

Poppy nodded emphatically. She was quieter now and Sylvia got the impression that she was absorbing the fact that her father was dead.

'At some point, just like we did with Matilda, we'll have a little ceremony for Daddy to wish him well on his journey. We can light some candles again and get his favourite food and flowers.'

Poppy swung her legs and frowned slightly.

Sylvia couldn't help wondering what thoughts and questions were swirling about in the little girl's head.

'Are we going to bury Daddy in the garden?'

Chrissy drew in a breath. 'No, it's only pets that get buried in the garden. Daddy will be buried in a special place, with other people.'

It occurred to Sylvia that Chrissy seemed to be assuming she would be deciding on the funeral arrangements, whereas a void second marriage wouldn't give her any rights. Perhaps it was the shock.

'Will we get to see him, then?' Poppy was still asking questions.

'I'm not sure yet. Probably not. It's different when it's a pet.' Chrissy let out a deep sigh. She looked exhausted. Traces of makeup had rubbed off and her eyes looked sunken in their sockets.

'What happens now? I mean, what on earth happens in this situation?' Chrissy turned to face Sylvia. 'I have absolutely no idea what to feel. What are we going to do?'

Sylvia was looking at a stranger, but she was also looking at a woman who had lost her husband, just like Sylvia had recently. Not in similar circumstances, but nevertheless Sylvia recognised the emotions that she herself still experienced. Expecting to hear Bill's key in the lock. Turning over in bed and forgetting he wasn't there. Moments of rage at him for leaving her.

She was retired now, of course, but she'd once had a social work client who found out her partner had another family. In that situation, the other family lived hundreds of miles away.

'I guess all you can do is take things one step at a time. Tracy will need to do the same, and the two of you can discuss what's going to happen.'

Sylvia wanted to bring Tracy into the conversation.

'It's not going to be easy for either of you but it's the only option. You'll both need to confer over things like the funeral.'

She didn't mention Robert's will. That was their business and could come later, but Sylvia was curious about whose decision it was for Robert to make a will – his or Chrissy's – and who the beneficiaries were. And whether he had another will with Tracy and the children as beneficiaries.

'And I would imagine that it will be helpful at some point for you both to sit down with a solicitor.'

That at least raised the subject of practicalities and would hopefully get Chrissy considering them.

'There's so much to think about. Thank you.'

Might Chrissy have had an inkling about Robert's infidelity? Sylvia sensed her shock and disbelief were genuine, but what if they were a protection mechanism?

She knew women often had a sense that their partners were being unfaithful, but, when confronted with the evidence, initially refused to believe it. It was the brain's way of protecting them from pain.

She needed to be careful about what she said in front of Poppy, but could she press Chrissy a little on whether she had any suspicions about Robert?

'I hope it's OK to ask. Where did you think Robert was yesterday?'

Tracy had been under the impression that he was away working and wasn't due back to the village until tomorrow.

'He was working,' Chrissy replied. 'He got up and went off to work just like he usually does. He covers a large area, so he stays in a hotel a few nights a week.'

It was what Tracy had said too.

'He said he was going to be away tonight and for the next two nights.'

As Chrissy spoke, it appeared the pennies were dropping and Sylvia waited as she gathered her thoughts and decided what to say.

'It's all falling into place. Did he tell me that he was going to be staying in a hotel when he was going to his *other family*?'

Sylvia knew it wasn't up to her to convey the information. 'Perhaps that's something you and Tracy can talk about? You probably both have questions along those lines.'

'Yes. Thank you.'

'I lost my husband recently, so I understand grief.' She watched as Poppy stroked her teddy. 'Did you have any

169

inkling about him ...' Sylvia stopped and used the phrase Chrissy had used, '... having another family?'

'No.' Anger darted across Chrissy's face. 'And I'm furious with him for putting us in this position. I'm always reading about those apps that enable you to check up on people, to find hidden files and locate trash folders. Key-logging software so you can get passwords.' She gestured to her phone. 'Geolocation apps to track people. I wish I'd used them and found out before we got married.'

'Of course.' There was something about Chrissy's description of this technology that made Sylvia want to ask more questions, but it would have to wait. 'Liam should be here any minute. Shall we go into the lounge and see how Tracy is?'

'Still licking her wounds, no doubt. Like this only affects her.'

Sylvia understood Chrissy's anger. 'She's suffering from grief and shock too.'

They were about to head into the lounge when the front door opened and Liam came into the kitchen. Concern spread over his face and his gaze landed first on Chrissy, then Sylvia.

'Where's Mum?'

'The lounge,' Sylvia replied. 'She refused to talk to Chrissy.'

'She's probably in shock.'

'She's not the only one,' said Chrissy. 'I don't know why you think it should be any tougher for your mother than for me.'

'I didn't say it was, but it's my mum I'm worried about. And my stepbrother and sister...' His sentence petered out.

'How are you coping with your stepfather's death?'

'It hasn't really hit me, to be honest. It's Mum I worry about. I knew Robert, obviously, but not well. I'm rarely at home. We do shifts at the garden centre and they're quite long. I'm usually knackered afterwards and I either come back here to see if Mum needs any help, or I go to Dad's and crash. Or I go out. But I don't tend to sit round, watching the telly with them. It's just not my thing.'

Liam was considerably older than Kieran and Emily and it made sense that he didn't spend a huge amount of time socialising with them. Sylvia thought he seemed like a nice young man, though, and it was probably useful for Tracy to have another male in the house, given that Robert was away for several days at a time. It was kind of Liam to help his mother out. A lot of young men wouldn't.

'Anyway, I left my phone charger here this morning. I'm going to nip upstairs and get it.' He hung his jacket on a peg by the front door. 'Then let's go in the lounge and get you two talking.'

'Can Emily come with us?' Poppy asked, holding out her teddy.

'Of course she can, sweetie,' Sylvia said softly. 'That's a pretty name.'

And too much of a coincidence, surely?

Chapter 23

2pm

When Dave arrived half an hour later, Ellie and Zoe had just started on the Richardson's holiday let in Deal. It was a four storey, three-bedroom town house near Deal Castle, with beams and an inglenook fireplace, overlooking the sea.

Ellie pushed the cloth round and round on the kitchen worktop. Sprayed cleaner. Round and round.

She felt shaky and it was a relief to have something physical to keep her mind off the note; to stop the constant questions about who the death threat could be from.

Zoe was hoovering the lounge.

The doorbell buzzed.

Zoe switched off the vacuum cleaner, lay the hose on the carpet and went onto the landing to buzz in her dad.

'We're upstairs,' she told him through the intercom. 'Second floor.'

A few moments later, Dave arrived and rushed over to Ellie. 'What happened? Are you OK?' He looked from Ellie to Zoe.

'Your friend, Ruby, was at the front door when Mum got home,' Zoe told her dad. 'Two hours later there's a death threat note on her windscreen.'

'You didn't tell me about Ruby,' Dave fired at Ellie.

'There's been rather a lot going on.' She told him what had happened.

'I don't know what she's playing at. She promised me she would leave you alone.'

Ellie shrugged. 'We were inside for a couple of hours after she left. I am not saying she put the note on my car. I didn't see anything.'

'You said she was looking for something...?'

Ellie told him how it had appeared. Peering around the plant pots. 'I didn't see her find anything. I think she only stopped because I arrived.'

'OK. I'll speak to her again. Find out what she was doing and tell her to leave you alone.'

'She also made a comment implying that she was meeting you for coffee,' Zoe added. 'Dad, are you sure she isn't dangerous?'

'Until last night, I would have said she wasn't but now I can't say for sure. However, it's not true that I was meeting her. I've been at work since first thing.' He looked at Ellie. 'I rang you earlier.'

'I know.'

Zoe told her dad she'd gone into the Windmill Inn to see if he was there.

Disappointment lodged itself on Dave's face and he swallowed. 'I suppose I can see why you wanted to know.' He changed the subject. 'Have you got the note?'

'It's on the worktop, over there. In the poo bag.' Ellie gestured to the kitchen. 'If you don't want to touch it, Zoe took a photo of it on her phone.'

She recounted what had happened. How they'd come out of the windmill, walked to the jeep and seen the note under one of the windscreen wipers.

Zoe showed her dad the image on her phone.

'*You need to learn when to quit*,' he read. '*It would be awful if you ended up like Robert Seale*.' He pursed his lips. 'I will find out who sent this.' He paced over to the window and looked out momentarily, then turned to face Ellie. 'You've got to keep yourself safe. Stay with Mum, Zoe, Finn, anyone...'

'I will.' Ellie could see Dave was finding it difficult to keep himself professional when the person who had received the death threat was her.

'Do you have any idea who this is from?' he asked.

'No.' Ellie closed her eyes. She felt sick.

'Does the wording or the phraseology ring any bells?'

'No.' Ellie pulled out a breakfast bar stool and perched on it, relieved to sit down.

He got his phone out and snapped a picture of the death threat. Read the message aloud.

'*You need to learn when to quit. It would be awful if you ended up like Robert Seale.*'

He marched across to the windows overlooking the sea.

'You need to learn when to quit,' he repeated, as though trying on the phrase.

He spun round to face Ellie. 'Who would want to say that sort of thing to you? Who wants you to *stop doing what*?'

Ellie threw her hands up in the air. 'Take your pick.' She felt exhausted.

'What does that mean?'

'Tell him, Mum,' Zoe prompted.

'Tracy and Sally asked us to look into Robert Seale's murder. I guess it could be someone who doesn't want us to do that.'

Dave groaned loudly. 'Like his killer, you mean? For God's sake, Ellie. This helping-others-in-spite-of-the-costs thing. It's why I fell in love with you but it's out of control. You've got to stop.'

'Don't tell me what to do.' Ellie retorted. 'Then there's whoever is poaching my cleaning customers. They might want me to stop cleaning.'

'What about this psycho, Ruby?' Zoe asked her mum. 'She clearly wants you to give up on Dad.'

'Give me your phone.' He held his hand out to Ellie. 'I'm putting a tracking app on it.'

'No. I don't want you checking up on me.'

'You mean, trying to make sure some idiot doesn't put an arrow in your back?'

'Let him, Mum. Don't be silly.'

'No.'

'This is a mess,' Dave said. 'I would never have thought Ruby would write a message like this, but then I was shocked when she sent you that text when we were in the woods. I haven't seen that side to her before. I'm extremely *concerned* to hear about her turning up at the windmill. It suggests she's—'

'... obsessed?' Zoe suggested.

He paused, thinking. 'Is there anyone else that you can think of who might want you to stop doing something?'

'No.'

'Are you sure?'

'I can't think of anyone. I haven't been keeping a... a list of who might want to kill me,' she spluttered.

It was then that the tears came.

Chapter 24

2.30pm

S ylvia was still at Tracy's house with Chrissy.

'Knock knock.' Sylvia peered round the door into Tracy's lounge and tried to sound light-hearted.

Tracy was curled up with her legs underneath her, a throw over her shoulders.

'Liam's home and Chrissy is still here. We thought we'd come in and join you. Is that OK?' She pushed the door open.

Liam wandered in and sat on the sofa next to his mum.

'I suppose.' Tracy didn't sound very enthusiastic.

'I'm worried about you,' Liam said.

'That's kind of you.' She ruffled his hair. 'I don't know what I would have done without your support over the last few years.' She let out a small, rather sad laugh. 'He's so grown up,' she announced to the room, presumably

179

nervous or emotional. 'It's sad to think that he used to be my baby. I guess that's what happens.' She laughed again. 'Anyway, ignore me. I'm just babbling.'

Sylvia thought about her grandson, Simon, and Zoe's boyfriend, Finn. They both seemed to be happy to spend time with her. And Dave, Simon and Zoe had remained close. They had the occasional row, but that was natural and it never lasted. If only she and Dave could heal their own rift. Hopefully, once she'd moved to Wootton permanently, that might come about.

She looked at Liam.

Perhaps it made a difference that he and his biological dad were close. It was a good sign that Liam wanted to spend time with both his mother and his father, and was comfortable enough to nip in and out as he wished.

Chrissy was sitting on a chair with Poppy on her knee.

Liam spoke. 'Now we've broken the ice—'

'We haven't.' Chrissy spat out the words.

Liam started again. 'Now we are all in the *same room*, would you like Sylvia and I to leave you to it?' He glanced at his mum and then Chrissy. 'It might be easier for the two of you to chat?'

Panic streaked over Tracy's features. 'Please don't go. I'm really not sure I can cope.'

Chrissy didn't speak.

Sylvia studied her face. Her jaw was clenched, and her cheek was twitching. There was resistance but not panic.

Sylvia checked her watch. She was keen to catch up with Ellie and Zoe but, at the same time, she didn't feel like she could abandon Tracy and Chrissy. 'OK, I will stay for a little bit but then I really must be going. Who would like to speak? Chrissy? Would you like to go first?'

'Thanks for letting me into your house,' said Chrissy tentatively.

'I didn't,' Tracy replied.

'You can blame me for that,' Sylvia said super-cheerfully. 'But it was probably a good idea though, don't you think? The two of you are going to have to talk to each other at some point, surely?'

'Did you really not know anything about me?' Tracy fired from the sofa.

'I've already answered that. Why on earth would I traipse all the way over here with my daughter and ask who you were if I knew?'

Chrissy had a point.

'Did you really not know Robert was already married?'

'I've answered that. No.'

'I don't believe you.'

'I don't care what you believe. If you didn't know, why should I?'

'What did he tell you about his previous relationships then?'

'That he was divorced.' Her voice rose in frustration. 'I was saying to Sylvia. I wish I'd used some of those tracking apps. Anything that would have prevented us from being in this situation.' She covered her face with her hand.

Sylvia's phone beeped in her bag. Hopefully nothing had happened to Ellie or Zoe.

Liam was watching the two women. From his expression, Sylvia guessed he was wishing he could be somewhere else.

'What about you?' Chrissy asked. 'Did you know about me? It's all very well for you to sit there feeling all wronged. Don't you think I feel exactly the same?'

'Of course, I didn't know about you. If I had, why on earth would I have been so surprised? After you left, I fainted. Do you think I pretended to do that?' Tracy tutted loudly.

'Look, rather than what *you* each did and didn't know,' Liam said, 'surely the point is how could *Robert* have done something like this?'

Sylvia waited, keen to see who her message was from.

The two women gradually began to talk to each other.

She watched and listened, and after fifteen minutes, she stood up. 'Is there anything else that you need me for?

Liam is here now. He said he doesn't have to go out for a while so he's happy to sit with you and make sure there aren't any fights.' She wanted to lighten the tone. 'I really need to get back to my family.'

'Sorry.' Tracy clambered off the sofa and went to give Sylvia a hug. 'You and Ellie have been amazingly kind.'

'Don't worry,' Sylvia replied. 'I understand.'

'As you say, we've just got to get on with it.'

Chrissy mouthed 'Thank you' at Sylvia.

'No problem.' Sylvia fished her mobile out of her bag. It was a text message from Zoe.

'What's difficult for me to get my head round is that I told Robert I wanted a divorce, and he begged me to give him another chance.' Tracy had found her voice now. 'I wish I'd said no, and then he could have left without a squeak, and for all we know this might not have happened.' She seemed to recalibrate. 'But, more importantly, our kids have just lost their dad and what has happened is tragic.'

'That's two things we can agree on,' Chrissy replied. 'Poor Poppy has had to sit here and listen to everything we've been saying. I agree that it would have been better if we'd both known about each other. If you didn't want to be married to Robert any more, it's such a shame that he couldn't have left and been with us full time instead of

183

this ridiculous timeshare thing that he seems to have been doing.'

Sylvia checked Liam's expression. He looked less than thrilled about his new role as referee.

She couldn't help wondering what was going to happen. Would the two women be able to work out an agreeable arrangement? How would Tracy's children react to the knowledge that their father had another family, and that they had a stepsister?

Sleuthing duties were one thing, but there was another reason why Sylvia wanted to get home.

She couldn't stop thinking about Ruby.

She had seen women like her come through Social Services, and Sylvia had a feeling that whatever she was up to, it wasn't about to stop.

She clicked on Zoe's text message.

'*Don't panic. We've given it to Dad. But someone left a death threat on Mum's car.*'

Chapter 25

4pm

Ellie and Zoe left the Richardson's together. Zoe escorted her mum back to the high street and headed off to her next cleaning job.

After the encounter with Ruby, finding the death threat note on the car and talking to Dave about it, Ellie was shaken. She fancied some fresh air but didn't want to go on her own.

She got her phone out and was about to call Sally when Sylvia's number came up. 'Sylvia?'

'Are you OK? I just got Zoe's text about the death threat. What the heck happened?'

Ellie explained.

'Don't go anywhere on your own,' Sylvia told her. 'I'm going to phone Dave. See if there's any news about who put it on your car.'

'He won't tell you anything.'

'I know but it'll let him know they need to find out.' She told Ellie she'd been with Chrissy and Tracy. 'This might be something or nothing and I nearly forgot.' She told Ellie that Chrissy had had a crushed bluebell on her boot tread.

'Hmm,' Ellie replied. 'That's a coincidence. Poppy had a bunch of bluebells in her hand when she arrived at Tracy's yesterday.'

'I suppose it *is* bluebell season. And Appledown aren't the only bluebell woods round here. That's not all though.' She told Ellie about Poppy's teddy.

'Emily's a popular name.'

'It is. And it's also the name of Tracy's daughter.'

'Another coincidence?'

'I think Chrissy needs to be a suspect. If she knew about Robert's first marriage, she could have a motive for getting rid of him. Rather than face the shame of the marriage being annulled and Robert face court.'

'Do you think she *did* know?'

Sylvia told Ellie about the tracking apps. 'It was most peculiar. The way she mentioned them, it was as if she was intimately familiar with them.'

'We need to find out where she was on the morning Robert was killed, then,' Ellie replied.

'You know the photograph you took of Liam Morris?'

'Yes.'

'I'm about to pop into the gym. Could you send it to me?'

'Sure. I'll do it now.' They said goodbye. Ellie found the image and sent it to Sylvia, then dialled Sally's number.

'Hey, Ells.'

'Bit short notice but I was just about to take Rebus out for a quick run and wondered if you and Luna wanted to come? After the death threat note on my car, Dave—'

'What death threat?'

Ellie brought Sally up to date.

'Is he investigating?'

She heard the concern in Sally's voice. 'He took the note for the lab.'

'Ells, this is serious.'

'I know. Dave's on at me not to go out on my own.'

'I'm with him on that, for now. Where were you thinking of going?'

'How about the woods? There might be something the police have missed. Would you mind coming with me?'

'Sure.'

'I'll nip home, get Rebus from the windmill. Shall I call round at yours in about ten minutes?'

'Fab. See you then.'

Five minutes later, Ellie had collected Rebus and was on her way back to Sally's house when, across the street, she spotted Nick Matthews shutting up the butcher's shop. Rebus, who treated everyone in the village like his long-lost friend, whimpered and pulled at his leash to go over.

Nick must have heard because he turned and crouched to greet Rebus. 'Hello, boy.' He fussed the dog's ears. 'How are you, Ellie? Isn't this business with Robert's murder absolutely awful? Sylvia told me that the Blix women are on the case again.' He chuckled. 'Good for you. Any idea yet who did it?'

'I believe the phrase is that we are "making inquiries".' She tugged on the dog's lead. 'Rebus, I'm not sure that Nick wants licking all over.' She laughed. 'I'm glad I bumped into you, actually. I was wondering whether it would be possible to see – or get a photo of – an arrow like the ones you had stolen recently? Sylvia realised that she should have asked you when she saw you, although I'm guessing your archery equipment is probably at the house rather than the shop?'

'Sure. Yes, it's all at home.' He lowered his voice and glanced about to check that nobody was listening. 'We do occasionally leave a bow and arrow in the flat above the shop, but after the burglary, we decided to make sure it's all kept locked up in the scullery at home. Safer that way.'

He was shaking his head in disbelief. 'I'll get Charlie to WhatsApp you a photo when I get home.'

'Do you happen to know if Robert annoyed anyone else with his shenanigans at the farm shop?'

'It's probably a bit easier for you to ask me who he *didn't* annoy. It wasn't just people whose businesses he was compromising. He got up to all sorts of unethical practices with his customers too. Not giving them the right change, overcharging them, changing the sell-by dates on the fresh produce. I know it's not the done thing to speak ill of the dead but, given you're investigating his murder, I'll be honest with you. That man didn't seem to have the slightest idea what common decency was.'

'Oh dear. Anyone in particular stand out? We're trying to identify all the people who might have had a motive for wishing him harm.'

'Actually, now you mention it, I had just arrived one day to collect some money from him. Of course, when I got there he didn't give it to me. The weird thing was Kathy from the baker's was there, and I could hear the two of them from the car park.'

'Shouting, you mean?'

He nodded. 'She was shrieking at him. Now, that's not normal for Kathy. Like you, I've known her for decades and she tends only to kick off when things get serious.'

'What happened?'

'I went charging in. I was worried about her being there on her own. And she was. She was screaming at him, "Why will anyone come to the baker's and buy from us when you are deliberately selling similar products at a much cheaper price?" and all he kept saying was, "That's not my problem. It's yours".'

'Sounds like a very similar story to yours and Pete's. What happened?'

'He said the same things to her as he said to us. Trying to make an honest buck. He could do anything he wanted. If she didn't like it, she'd have to lump it. Ugh.' He shook his head. 'What's interesting though is, shortly after that he stopped selling any baked goods, plants and meat.'

'Literally all?'

'Uh-huh. So, something Kathy said or did – or her husband or lawyer – must've changed Robert's mind.'

'Did you ever find out what it was?'

'No. And Kathy never mentioned it either. I'm sure she'll tell you more about what happened, if you ask her.'

'I think I will. Thanks.' Ellie sensed that Kathy wasn't a suspect, but they needed to know what made Robert stop his unethical behaviour.

'Shortly after that, Robert left the farm shop and Brian and Lily sold it.'

'Interesting. Before I go, Linda replied to my Facebook post. She said you've had a leaflet through the door recently, offering cleaning services.' She told him about her customers cancelling their contracts.

'We did. Last week. Linda mustn't have realised I chucked it in the recycling. If Charlie hasn't emptied the bin, it should still be there. I'll have a look and, if it is, I'll drop it round. Alright?'

'Cheers, Nick. Much appreciated. They must be new as I've Googled and nothing comes up except Blix Blitz – and some national company pretending to be local.'

Tucking the phone back in her jacket pocket, she carried on up the high street, past all the shops towards Sally's house, all the while trying to fend off the thought that someone was poaching her customers and someone wanted her dead.

Chapter 26

4.15pm

Sylvia stood at reception, trying to avoid the mirrors which were everywhere.

'I can't allow you in, I'm afraid, unless you're a member,' the young man on reception told her. He had a crew-cut and didn't bother looking up from his keyboard.

The weights room was to the right of the desk. Sylvia could make out benches and shiny objects.

This was going to need some amateur dramatics.

'It's a *family emergency*,' Sylvia whispered. 'I'm his gran. I'll be two minutes.' She walked towards the glass entry barriers. 'Let me through, would you?'

'I'm not meant to, but just this once. Andy will be in the corner with the weights.'

When Sylvia pushed the double doors open, she was overwhelmed by the bright lights and thumping beat of the music in the gym.

She didn't have long.

She scanned the room.

There he was. Tall, thickset.

She scuttled over.

'Alright, Grandma.' Andy had seen her coming. 'Come for a training session, have you?'

'Actually, I've come to talk to you about your early morning dog walks in Appledown Woods. Aren't you meant to keep your greyhound on the lead?' Sylvia didn't know this for a fact, but it was worth bluffing.

Andy's face was like thunder. His phone beeped in his pocket. 'What's it got to do with you? Are you from Busybodies Anonymous?'

'I won't tell anyone if you tell me who you saw in the woods the morning Robert Seale was killed.'

'Are you with that woman what asked me all those questions at the petrol station? The copper's wife?' He moved a barbell.

'That's us. I'm his mother. And the answer is...?'

'I don't know who it was. Never seen her before. She had dark brown hair and was wearing a long red parka with a furry hood.'

'That it?'

'She also had a brown Labrador in the car. But, no, she wasn't carrying a bow and arrow when I saw her.'

Chapter 27

4.30pm

E llie arrived at Sally's house slightly later than she'd suggested. She rang the bell and watched Rebus squeal and squirm while he waited for the door to open.

'Sorry,' Ellie said when Sally appeared. 'I got talking to Nick. I'll tell you all about it once we get walking.'

'Not a problem. It gave me a chance to take in a skirt for Gladys Blackman.'

Sally was the village dressmaker.

'She's lost weight, poor thing.' Sally let Luna go ahead and closed the front door behind her. She took out a Chubb key and inserted it in the lock. 'I'm being more careful about security now, are you?'

'Yes, we've moved our spare key.'

Soon the two friends slipped into their easy rhythm, catching up on news.

They were quickly on the village green. Both dogs pricked up their ears and strained at their leads when they saw and heard the farmer's sheep in the new pen, ready and waiting for the windmill open day.

'I'm looking forward to Aidan and Jane's wedding party on Sunday afternoon,' Sally said. 'I know Pete's already helping Bob and Finn outside. Do you need a hand indoors?'

'Thank you. Sylvia has been baking for months – so yes, please. At this rate, we're going to need to put up about fifty trestle tables for all her baked products.' She chuckled. They'd all been enjoying the mouth-watering smells from the oven and regular sampling opportunities. 'There's always a split between people who want to see round the windmill and those who want to do the outdoor stuff.'

Once they had left the green, they crossed Pennypot Lane and walked along the footpath beside the church towards Appledown Woods. Soon Luna and Rebus were scurrying about in the undergrowth and pelting along the path, sniffing things out in the bluebells.

As they nattered, they entered the clearing and followed the dogs towards Rattling Folly. In the late afternoon light, the bricks had a grey hue.

'Have you had a chance to talk to Pete?' Ellie asked.

'Yes. We had a long conversation after you and he spoke, and he told me about the leak and the difficulty with finding a plumber. He realised he'd worried me.'

Ellie heard the relief in her friend's voice.

High above them, the sound of a woodpecker rattled through the trees. They stopped to listen.

A twig snapped behind them.

Ellie froze. *'What was that?'* She grabbed Sally's sleeve.

'Didn't hear anything.'

Ellie spun round and scanned the glade.

Just Rebus and Luna, darting about.

She let go of Sally's jacket. 'Probably the dogs. Or me being jumpy.' She carried on walking. 'You were talking about Pete.'

'Yeah,' Sally replied. 'It was handy that Nick was around to help him. What's troubling though is that when Pete inspected the pipe, it was clear it had been sabotaged.'

Ellie slowed in her tracks. 'Really? What will that involve? Does it mean an investigation?'

'So I gather.'

'Does Pete have any idea who might've done it?'

Sally was nodding. And even though they were in the woods with no one around, she looked about and whispered, 'He's convinced it was Robert Seale.'

Ellie gasped.

This was it.

This was what Pete was being cagey about.

'When did he come to that conclusion?'

Sally winced as she spoke. 'As soon as he saw the pipe.'

'You mean before the wedding?'

She nodded.

'Has he told the police?'

'I don't think so. He's worried it's going to make him a suspect.'

'But why would it?' Ellie asked. 'Robert would have been dead by the time the leak happened.'

Sally seemed perplexed. 'I don't understand the ins and outs of it.'

Something still wasn't right. 'Do you—'

'Did you hear that?' Sally whispered.

'Someone coughed,' Ellie whispered back. *'I swear. Over there.'* She pointed towards the silver birch trees by the folly. *'C'mon. This is freaking me out. Let's go back.'* Her heart was hammering in her chest.

'I agree,' Sally said. 'Luna, Rebus. Come.'

They strode out in silence, retracing their steps, the dogs in tow. Once they were back on the main path, they began talking freely again.

'What the heck was that?' Sally was out of breath. 'Some kids up at the folly?'

'Let's hope that's all it was.'

'Has Dave taken the death threat in for forensic testing?'

'Yes.'

'What were you going to ask me?' Sally said.

'... if you feel better after talking to Pete?'

'Ye-es.'

'That sounds like "no".'

'There's still something he's not being honest about. I can't stop thinking about the leaves on his boots.'

Ellie remembered how clean they were by the time she saw him.

'I keep thinking – I've never seen Pete so angry as the last few days,' Sally whispered. 'What if he went to meet Robert in the woods and things got out of control?'

The dogs came bounding over, somersaulting and play-fighting. Rebus had something in his mouth.

'What if Pete and Robert had a fight or he lost his temper?' Sally asked.

It was a possibility.

Nick had said Pete did archery. Perhaps his patience had worn out? He *had* tried to reason with Robert over the farm shop and it hadn't worked. Robert had called the bluff of all of them: Pete, Nick and Kathy. And he'd got away with it. If he'd then caused damage at the garden centre, maybe Pete had snapped?

They were going to have to speak to him again.

Just at that moment, Rebus dropped what he'd found and used his nose to push it at Ellie. His usual trick to get her to throw it or play tug-of-war.

Ellie picked it up.

'What is it?' Sally asked.

It was a moulded strip of brown leather with four straps.

Ellie turned it over. 'Looks like some sort of guard.'

Chapter 28

6pm

Zoe must have spotted Ellie coming up the drive to the windmill because she opened the front door as her mum was scurrying up the path with Rebus.

'Thank goodness you're home,' she said. 'I've been worried sick.'

A golden cockerpoo puppy hurled herself at Ellie, wriggling like a worm and squealing like she was about to die with excitement and urgency.

When Ellie looked up from the bundle of fur, Sylvia was standing next to Zoe. 'Everything OK?'

'Thanks, yes.' Ellie felt a whoosh of love for her family. 'Don't worry. I was with Sally the whole time.' Ellie handed Rebus' lead to Zoe and scooped up puppy Agatha.

'Gran has made a feast,' said Zoe excitedly as she unclipped Rebus' lead. 'I've already tasted the new Nigella apple crumble. It's proper lush.'

'I added a bit of ground clove and doubled the cinnamon,' Sylvia said, 'and put some extra vanilla in the custard.'

'Hurry up, you guys,' Simon shouted through from the lounge. 'We're waiting to open the Prosecco.'

'Dad can't make it.' Zoe screwed up her face in disappointment. 'Something to do with work.'

'He would've come if he could.' Ellie put Agatha down, closed the door and hung up her coat.

In the kitchen, Sylvia, Finn, Simon and Jen were sitting around the wooden table. In the centre were two bottles of fizz and seven flute glasses. Food, family, dogs. Their lovely home. It was a welcome relief after Robert's murder and the death threat.

Ellie joined the group.

Simon was pouring the wine. His beard had grown since she'd seen him last. It always struck her how like Dave he was in build. Solid, muscular and tall.

Was she imagining it or was there a sense of excitement amongst them all?

Simon passed glasses to everyone present. 'Mum?' he said as he passed Ellie hers.

There was one empty glass.

Dave's.

'I've been waiting to do this since Christmas,' Simon smiled over at his mum. 'And here we finally are.' He turned his attention to Jen, who had a black baker boy cap on top of a blonde pixie cut. 'Babe, will you do me the greatest honour... and marry me?'

Jen's face flushed pink. 'Yes, yes, yes.'

Ellie gasped. 'I had no idea this was coming. Come here, you two.' Ellie enveloped Simon and Jen in a huge hug. When she let go a few moments later, she gazed into her son's face and held out an arm for Zoe. 'In case I haven't told you lately, I am so very proud of you and your sister. And now another gorgeous woman will join the Blix clan.'

'Oh, Mumm,' Simon said, beaming from ear to ear. 'What are you like?'

───ele───

Once the celebration was over, Simon and Jen took puppy Agatha home and Zoe and Finn nipped to the pub to meet Charlie and Liam. Sylvia stuffed two batches of scones in the oven and settled down with her feet up in front of the TV.

Ellie gathered up her work diary and phone and went upstairs to her bedroom to ring Jeff Klepper about the call centre's cleaning. She drew the curtains and sat at her dressing table. The lamp cast a cool glow over the white walls and bed linen.

She dialled Jeff but the call went to voicemail.

Ellie had planned what she wanted to say and left a brief message. '*This is Ellie here from Blix Blitz cleaners. I got your message saying that you would like to give notice. Is it possible for you to give me a quick call back? I understand that you've made your decision, so please don't worry that I'm going to try and persuade you to do anything that you don't want. It's simply that it would be useful for me to understand why you no longer would like us to do your cleaning. If there is something that we need to address at Blix Blitz, I would love to have the opportunity of doing that, as this is a family business and I've been running it for fifteen years. I do hope you don't mind me giving you a call and I look forward to hearing from you.*'

She flicked through her diary and found the contact details for the Langs. Hopefully, they might explain their reasons.

She pressed 'dial' and waited to see if they would answer.

'Hi, Ellie.' It was Mr Lang.

Ellie said pretty much the same thing as she had in her message to Jeff. Then added, 'Earlier in the week, Nick Matthews said he'd received a leaflet from someone called something like Wootton Cleaners. I just wondered if you'd had a leaflet from them too and whether this was the company you decided to move your cleaning to?'

'That's them, yes. Wootton Cleaners. We thought they were you.'

Ellie explained they weren't.

'Sorry, Ellie. We've been away for two weeks. Been playing catch-up ever since we got back. The leaflet implied it was you, just under new branding.'

'Can you remember what it said?'

'Something about being a local business who's just rebranded. They mentioned changing their payment terms in order to modernise the business. That's why they were asking people to cancel and re-sign up.'

That was underhand. Who was doing this? Surely, they must realise they were going to put Ellie out of business?

'I suspect we didn't look at the leaflet closely enough,' Mr Lang continued.

'Do you mind me asking what payment terms they are offering?'

'Hold on a moment. Let me ask my wife. She dealt with them.' In the background Ellie heard, 'Darling? Do you remember how much Wootton Cleaners are charging? It seems like somebody is trying to impersonate Ellie's company and pinch her customers.'

There was a woman's voice.

Ellie waited. She had been lucky, being the only cleaning company in the area for all this time.

'Ellie?' The woman came on the phone. 'This is Alice. I'm so sorry. I thought you'd changed your branding and restructured. Their prices are cheaper than yours, but with living costs so high, lots of businesses are doing it. Presumably, this is a scam?'

'I think so. And a clever one in many ways. I have been Googling them for a couple of days. Can't find anything.'

'I did notice that they didn't clean our place the way you used to, and I was going to ask you about it if it continued.'

'Did you recognise any of the cleaners?'

'No. I thought that you'd perhaps expanded and taken on new staff, and were in the process of training them all up.'

'No.'

'We're extremely sorry about this, Ellie. We wouldn't have dreamt of changing companies. I'll have a chat with my husband. We would obviously like to go back to using Blix Blitz, if you'll have us. This other company better not insist on holding us to a notice period after their underhand tactics.'

'Thank you. We've got additional staff so we can restart your jobs whenever you're ready. Could you photograph the leaflet and email it to me so I can see what they're saying?'

'Of course.'

Ellie gave Alice her email address and rang off with a sinking feeling in her stomach.

A man had been killed.

Someone had sent her a death threat.

Someone was impersonating her business and poaching her customers.

Thank goodness the Langs had been so amenable. Was Jeff Klepper at the call centre going to be?

Ellie climbed onto her bed and lay back, staring up at the ceiling. She reached for her phone and dialled Dave's number. It rang twice and his voicemail clicked in, as though someone had bounced the call. His familiar voice in his outgoing message brought a lump to her throat.

'Just me,' she said. 'Wondering if there's any news on who left the death threat on my car. The rival cleaning company is... oh, never mind.' She rang off. Checked her email. Nothing from Alice Lang yet.

Downstairs, she could hear the TV. She was trying to decide between joining Sylvia, having a bath or popping out for some air. She padded back downstairs.

'The scones smell delicious.'

They were cooling on the rack.

'Don't they? I'm rather pleased with them. The open day guests are going to love them.'

Ellie smiled. Sylvia had put super-human effort into making the open day successful. 'Do you fancy a quick stroll over to the duck pond?' She told Sylvia about the earlier noises in the woods.

'I'll get my jacket. I hope the police catch this person soon.'

A few moments later, they were crossing Pennypot Lane. The area around the Windmill Inn was busy. People were bustling about, getting in and out of cars and calling after each other.

They stepped over the metal chain fencing and onto the green.

To Ellie, it all seemed so loud.

The light of the moon splashed onto the wet grass and the pond. In their pen, the lambs and their mothers bleated contentedly. It was hard to believe there was a murderer in the village again.

And that someone wanted her dead.

She shuddered.

The two women made their way over to the bench by the pond, discussing Ellie's conversation with the Langs.

'We'll get it sorted.' Sylvia put her arm round Ellie and gave her a squeeze. 'Don't worry.'

Her words brought a lump to Ellie's throat. When she and Dave had separated, the business had weighed heavily on her, and it was a relief to know she wasn't on her own.

'Thank you.'

On the water, one of the sets of ducklings was swimming along behind their mum, innocently quacking and paddling away with their tiny feet. Ellie tracked their path, enjoying concentrating on something nurturing. 'I love this spot. It's so peaceful.'

'It really is.'

The mother duck and her ducklings clambered up the bank and started pecking away at the mud beside the pond.

Ellie was entranced. Every year there were ducklings here, but this year there seemed to be more than ever.

'By the way, I haven't had the chance to tell you about the woman Andy Morris saw in the woods,' Sylvia said. She told Ellie about her brown hair and long red parka.

'It's got to have been Chrissy Seale, surely?' said Ellie. 'If she was in the woods just after Robert was killed, she *could* have been there earlier.'

'... hence the bluebells on her boots.'

'I wonder if the police know.'

Ellie's phone pinged in her pocket, announcing a WhatsApp message. Her heart sank as she was jerked back into reality.

Please, not another message from Ruby.

Or a death threat straight to her mobile.

She was tempted to ignore it, to enjoy these precious moments under the moon, watching the ducklings hoover up food.

But it could be Zoe or the call centre manager.

She pulled her phone from her jeans pocket, swiped the screen and took a deep breath.

The digit combination was familiar.

Ruby's.

Anger swept over Ellie.

Enough was enough.

She tapped on the message.

It was text in a photograph.

'*I hope you realise that the rubbish Dave is telling you is just to be kind. He doesn't have the heart to tell you the truth.*

The fact is it's been over between you two for a long time. You just don't see it. You don't know when to quit, do you? Ruby.'

Ellie let out a scream.

The chicks scattered.

'What is it?' Sylvia asked.

Ellie clicked out of WhatsApp. Her impulse was to fling her phone into the pond so that Ruby would never be able to text her again.

When she got home, she would ask Zoe or Finn to block Ruby's number. Stop her from sending any more vile messages.

It was too much.

On top of everything else, now she had Ruby trying to make her walk away from Dave.

'You don't know when to quit.'

Had Ruby sent the death threat too?

She re-opened the app to screenshot the image. But it had disappeared. There was just a message in italics saying, *Opened*, with a circle of dashes to the left.

This was getting scarier by the moment.

Ellie turned and faced Sylvia.

Ruby had gone to the trouble of sending her a message which no one could now read.

Chapter 29

8.45pm

Ellie got up from the bench and, with Sylvia following, was quickly striding across the green towards Dave's flat. Onto Pennypot Lane, along the high street, down the alley beside the florist and into the road which led to Goose Meadow, where Dave lived.

Ellie flew up the path to Dave's front door and rang the buzzer.

'I'll wait here,' Sylvia said.

After a few minutes, Ellie heard shoes clomping on the hard floor in the hall and Dave opened the front door.

'Ellie.' He looked flustered. 'What are you doing here?' His shirt collar was open and his hair was messed up.

'I've just had another message. Can I come in?'

'*A death threat?*'

'No. One of those View Once things from Ruby. Can I come in or not?' Ellie felt cold. 'For goodness' sake.' She barged past Dave and into the hallway.

'You can't...'

Ellie carried on talking to him as she walked down the hall towards the kitchen and lounge. 'That's twice in one day. First, she turns up at my house, now this.'

The lounge door was open and the fire was on. As she approached the room, a different smell hit her nostrils.

Perfume.

Once she got to the doorway, she stopped dead. Because, sitting on the sofa, looking as smug as anything, was Ruby.

White T-shirt, jeans, shoes off and legs tucked under her on the sofa.

'We must stop meeting like this.' Ruby's voice dripped with sarcasm.

Ellie opened her mouth to speak but no words would come out.

Ruby raised her glass. 'Cheers.'

'That's... what... I was trying to tell you,' Dave stammered.

'What is *she* doing here?'

She looked from Dave to Ruby and back to Dave again.

'She wanted to...' Dave's words petered out. He closed his eyes and let out a long, slow sigh. 'She wanted to *talk*.'

'I've obviously got things wrong—'

His hair.

The shirt.

His furtive air.

The wine.

'Yes, you have,' said Ruby. '*Again.*'

'Ells, please. It's not what you think.'

That old chestnut.

Ellie had been an idiot. Ruby had been telling the truth all along. First Andrea, now her.

Ruby was right. Things *had* been over between them for a long time, and it was about time she accepted it.

'That's exactly what you said about Andrea. And, silly me, I believed you.'

'I'll call you tomorrow.'

'No. You won't. Just forget it. I can't believe you missed your son's engagement for *this*.' She spun round and stomped out of the room, back to the front door and outside to Sylvia.

Somehow, she made it back down the path to the gate, yanked it open and strode out into the road, muttering under her breath, 'How could he?' she shouted at Sylvia. 'How the hell could he?'

Dave was calling after Ellie.

She kept walking.

'Ellie, wait,' Sylvia was pleading now too and running after her.

In her rage, Ellie stumbled up the kerb into the alley. Gravity tipped her forward and she fell and thumped down on her front, breath shooting out of her, face hitting the stony ground of the path.

Seconds later, pain consumed her.

She lay there on the ground for a few moments, shocked. Then pulled her legs underneath her body, managing to sit up and perch on the kerb.

Her hand rose to her smarting cheek. To her nose.

Ouch.

It was wet.

Sticky.

And very slowly, as Ruby's victorious face came into her mind, her large brown eyes, her sneering manner, Ellie began to cry.

Chapter 30

9.30pm

Half an hour later, Ellie was back home at the windmill, on the sofa in her pyjamas.

'Here you go.' Sylvia handed Ellie a mug of hot chocolate. 'Please don't feel you have to defend him or walk on eggshells. If my son is messing around with this Ruby woman, he's an idiot. I'm tempted to go back round there and give him a piece of my mind.'

'Please don't.'

'Same with me, Mum,' Zoe said. 'Say what you need to.'

Zoe still had her jacket on. She and Finn had dashed back to the windmill from the pub. She was applying antiseptic spray to the grazes on her mum's nose and cheek. 'She wanted to *talk*?'

'That's what he said.' Ellie felt drained of all energy. She took a sip of Sylvia's hot chocolate, tasting a hint of something else amid the sugar. 'Wow. That's got a kick to it. What did you put in it?'

'A shot of cognac that I found in your baking cupboard.'

'Thank you.'

'Why was she drinking wine?' Zoe added.

'No idea.' Ellie's nose was throbbing and her cheek was smarting. 'On a different subject... several people in the village have had leaflets from this new cleaning company apparently. They all assumed it was Blix Blitz under a new brand—'

'*Leaflets.*' Sylvia threw her hands up in the air. 'That reminds me. While we were out, Charlie put their leaflet through the letter box.' She slid off the sofa and scuttled off into the kitchen, returning a few moments later with an A5 sheet. 'Here we are.'

She read out the text:

'*Let local company, Wootton Cleaners, do all those tasks that you hate. Cleaning the oven and fridge, defrosting the freezer, changing the beds, making those mirrors and windows sparkle. We are the same company you've always trusted, just with a new pricing structure to reward your loyalty.*'

'What does that mean? "The same company you've always trusted"?' Zoe looked furious. 'Are these people new and pretending not to be, or are they national, pretending to be local?' Zoe was already on her phone, scrolling through her internet browser.

'Can I have a look?' Ellie held out her hand.

Zoe took a quick snap of the leaflet with her phone and passed it to her mum.

Finn sat down next to Ellie on the sofa and the two of them took a few minutes to read through the text.

'I can't say for sure,' he said, 'as we don't know who's running this new company, but it looks to me as though those are stock images off the internet.'

'Yep,' Zoe replied. 'Look. I've just Googled 'Cleaners Wootton' and clicked on images. The one they've used comes up free on Photostock. I had to scroll down a bit but it's there.' She held up her phone so that her mum and boyfriend could see.

'Lots of people use stock images in their advertising,' Finn said, 'but it's usually when they don't have any photos of their own to use. Bob uses pictures of him and me on the Campbell Tree Surgery website. He shows the two of us working, because he wants local people to see that it's us. They know and trust us from the village.'

'Perhaps that is exactly why these Wootton Cleaners people haven't used photos of them?' Zoe suggested. 'Maybe they don't *want* people to know who they are?'

'Except customers are going to find that out once the cleaners turn up at their properties for work,' Sylvia said.

'I'm guessing that it's not the cleaners' faces that they want to hide. It's more likely to be the faces of the owners of the company. If they're new, they might not have got round to organising on-site photos yet.'

'That's a really good point,' Ellie said to Sylvia. 'It's odd that there's no contact number, just an e-mail address. I know that's the modern way, but it's not very personal. A lot of people want to pick up the phone and speak to a person.'

'I can vouch for that,' Sylvia said. 'I answer a lot of telephone enquiries from cleaning customers who don't use email.'

'Finn, you have an e-mail address that doesn't use your name.' Zoe put her hand on her boyfriend's forearm. 'Do you want to e-mail these people? Pretend to be a customer and get some information out of them? Ask who the owners are?' She read out the e-mail address.

'That's a good idea.' He tapped out a quick message on his phone and pressed 'send'. 'When you Googled cleaners in Wootton, Zo, what did you get?'

'All I got was Blix Blitz, then a company in Dover, one in Sandwich, and some national company, offering cleaning services everywhere.'

'That's exactly what I found when I looked,' said Ellie.

Zoe was staring at her phone. 'I'm looking at the Blix Blitz website now and these Wootton Cleaners people have definitely used similar colours on their leaflets. Our brand colours are deep pink and a bluey-green. They've used a slightly lighter pink and turquoise. OK, so it's not identical but, let's face it, it's very similar.'

'Yes. Much too similar to be a coincidence.' Sylvia was not impressed. 'The thing is, if you want to set up a business which offers similar services to an existing one in the village, by all means do it. But do it fairly and ethically. Don't try and pretend you are the existing business.'

'I agree,' Ellie said.

'Do they really think people aren't going to find out and feel tricked?' Sylvia continued. 'We all know that introductory offers can be appealing, but if you deliberately try and undercut other people's prices, you'll put them out of business.' She had a tea towel in her hand, and flung it over the back of a chair and stomped off towards the kitchen.

Zoe was still Googling on her phone. 'Hang on a sec. It looks like what these people are doing could be illegal.' She continued to scroll. 'There are dozens of articles on here about business impersonation.'

Dave had mentioned this.

'We need to screenshot all our searches for possible evidence. If these people are breaking the law, we might be able to stop them.'

Chapter 31

10.30pm

Ellie and Zoe had gone to bed. Sylvia, however, was wide awake. She was livid about Wootton Cleaners and wanted to do something to help. Before Christmas, she'd seen how much of a toll it had taken on Ellie to run Blix Blitz and clean all day. Since then, Sylvia had watched Ellie build the business to the stage now where she only had to do *some* of the physical work herself, and Sylvia was *not* going to stand back while someone took that away from her.

She fetched Ellie's laptop from the office and logged on. Sylvia wasn't great on the internet and found it tiring and frustrating but had needed to use it a lot when she was a social worker.

Something was bothering her.

Both Ellie and Zoe had found a national cleaning company when they were looking for local ones, and it got her thinking: the social services' digital teams often discovered that websites were diverted. Sometimes this was because domains had expired or because a trading name had changed. But it was often used when people actively wanted to obscure identities.

She was scrolling away when a knock at the door made her jump.

The clock on the mantlepiece said 10.30pm. Who could it be at this time of night?

Zoe was in bed, so it couldn't be her having forgotten her keys.

There was a second knock. More urgent this time.

Sylvia placed the laptop on the coffee table and got up. She crept over to the front door and peered through the security hole.

It was Dave.

'Ellie?' He shouted. 'I need to talk to you.' His words were slurred.

Sylvia quickly unbolted the door and flung it open. 'Shh,' she hissed at her son. 'You'll wake up the whole house.'

'Please can you get Ellie? I need to speak to her.' His jacket was hanging off one shoulder.

'She's in bed. Which – by the looks of it – is where you should be.'

'Please don't have a go at me, Mum. Just get Ellie, would you? Or let me in.'

For a few moments, Sylvia didn't know what to do. Wanting to protect Ellie was one thing but making decisions on her behalf was different, and much as she wanted to tell Dave to go home, it didn't seem fair on either of them.

'Wait out there. I'll go and see if she's awake.' Sylvia closed the door quietly and padded up the stairs. She crept across the landing and put her ear to Ellie's door.

Silence.

She listened again, to be certain.

Sylvia was about to go back downstairs and tell Dave to go home when she heard Ellie crying.

She had known Ellie for over thirty-five years, from when Dave had first asked if she could come for tea after school.

They had been childhood sweethearts.

She had to tell Ellie that Dave was downstairs. She couldn't let her cry herself to sleep if he had an explanation which could take some of her hurt away.

She tapped on the door and eased it open. 'Ellie, lovey? Dave is downstairs, asking to talk to you.'

'What about?'

'I don't know. What would you like me to tell him? Do you want to talk to him?'

'No.' She let out a sob. 'Tell him to go away.'

'Are you sure?'

'Yes. I'm not listening to him anymore.'

'OK.' She closed the door with a heavy heart. Opened it again. 'Are you really sure?'

'Tell him to go away.'

Back at the front door, when Sylvia opened it, Dave was leaning against the outside of the windmill.

'Sorry. She doesn't want to listen.'

He closed his eyes and let his head rest back on the external wall of the windmill.

He looked awful.

'I've messed up, Mum. I don't know what to do.'

'I don't know what you've done, but I care about you both and I don't want to be the go-between. I know it's hard, but you'll have to wait until she wants to listen.'

'I think I'm going to throw up.' He was standing by Ellie's potted plants.

She tutted. 'Excellent. That will do the plants a world of good.'

'Please can you tell Ellie that—?'

'No. I'm not passing on messages. I've been in the confidante situation before, and it's a constant worry about whether to pass things on or keep quiet. If you want to talk to her, you'll have to persuade her to listen.'

'How can I get her to listen when she won't talk to me?'

Sylvia sighed. It was hard seeing Dave in pain. 'I don't know. You'll have to figure it out.'

'I'm going home,' he said huffily.

'It's probably best. Night, love.' Sylvia watched her son stagger back down the drive into Pennypot Lane.

It wasn't like Dave to drink this much. He was going to have a dreadful hangover in the morning.

She went back inside the windmill and closed the front door, sliding the two security bolts across. What a peculiar day it had been. Ellie's death threat. Simon and Jen's engagement. Agatha the puppy. Ruby and Dave. The rival cleaning company.

And now Dave turning up drunk.

What had he meant by 'messing up'?

She had a feeling she wasn't going to sleep well.

She made a cup of camomile tea and returned to the laptop. The screensaver had come on, so she entered Ellie's password and carried on scrolling through the list of cleaning businesses. She clicked on the company in Dover and clicked on the 'Areas Covered' tab. The website talked about covering Dover and the surrounding area. It then listed what these were: Eythorne, Ringwould and Kingsdown.

Wootton wasn't mentioned at all. Nor was Deal.

Next, she clicked on the national company that Ellie and Zoe had both found and this time scrolled down to the bottom of the page to see if their registered offices were listed.

BluePrint Franchises Ltd.

Unit 283, Princess Margaret Industrial Estate,

Wincheap,

Canterbury, Kent.

BluePrint. She was tired, but the name was familiar. She was sure she'd heard it in the past couple of days.

She sipped her tea and sat back on the sofa, letting the laptop rest on her legs. If someone had mentioned it, where had she been and who had she talked to?

The wedding.

Tracy.

BluePrint was the franchise company Robert Seale had been working for. That must mean he was selling cleaning franchises.

'Holy cow,' she said to Rebus. 'Robert was involved with this too.'

Chapter 32

DAY 3 – Saturday, 7am

The next morning, Ellie was downstairs before anyone else. She let Rebus out in the back garden. Saturday was usually one of her favourite days of the week because Lower Wootton had its market on the village green, but she hadn't slept well, and had, of course, dreamt about Dave and Ruby again. Her brain was already bombarding her with questions and images.

Why had Ruby been at Dave's flat last night?

And why had he come round to the windmill so late?

But the Dave situation would have to wait. She needed to focus on keeping herself safe and finding Robert's killer. It seemed almost certain that Chrissy Seale had been in the woods the morning Robert was killed. They needed to talk to her again.

She filled the kettle and, as water sprayed over the draining board, an image flashed through her mind of Pete's sabotaged pipe and the damaged stock at the garden centre. After walking in the woods with Sally, she hadn't had the chance of following up on that.

She needed to make a list of people to investigate further, starting with Chrissy and Pete.

While Rebus was in the garden and the kettle was boiling, she shuffled into the lounge in search of a notepad. Sylvia had left the laptop surrounded by Post-its. A fluorescent yellow one was stuck to the left of the track pad.

On it, Sylvia had written '*BluePrint Ltd and national cleaning company are connected. Was Robert Seale selling cleaning franchises?*'

BluePrint was definitely the name of Robert's franchise operation. Was she understanding it right? She re-read Sylvia's note. BluePrint and the national cleaning company that had come up in their internet searches were connected. And Robert was involved?

Wow.

That certainly put a different complexion on things. And...oh, God, it could put Ellie in the frame. The police might think she wanted revenge on Robert or had financial motives for killing him.

Ellie ran to the back door and called for Rebus to come in.

He tore towards her, like he always did, as though he hadn't seen her for a week.

She grabbed up one of the notepads and a pen.

The two of them pounded up the spiral staircase and across the landing to Sylvia's room. Ellie knocked and put her head round the door. 'Morning. Can I come in? I've just seen your Post-it note about Robert's franchises.'

Over the past four months, Sylvia's moisturiser, perfume and hairbrush had replaced Simon's technology and stinky trainers in his old room.

'Morning,' Sylvia grunted. 'Yes.'

Rebus pushed past Ellie's legs, squealing, and jumped on Sylvia's bed.

'That was genius, finding the address for BluePrint last night. It wouldn't surprise me one bit if Robert was linked to this company that's been trying to undercut me and poach my customers. Would it you?'

'Not in the least.' Sylvia let out a deep sigh. She sat up and swung her legs over the edge of the bed.

'I've never shot an arrow in my life so hopefully that will stop them from considering me a suspect.'

'All the same, it would be good to wrap this up. I'm convinced Chrissy killed Robert.'

'She's definitely on the suspect list, isn't she?' Ellie told Sylvia about the pipe damage at the garden centre.

'And Pete thinks *Robert* sabotaged it? We should speak to Pete too then.'

'Yes. And with everything that happened yesterday, I forgot to mention that Nick said Kathy from the bakery had a run-in with Robert about the farm shop as well. So, we'll need to speak to her too. Rule her out.' Ellie perched on the edge of Sylvia's bed and wrote 'Chrissy, Pete, Kathy, Finn' on the notepad. 'I can't wait to find out if Finn's had a reply to his enquiry about cleaning.'

'The company must have administrative support,' Sylvia replied. 'It can't just have been Robert on his own, surely?'

'We'll soon find out. I wonder if Tracy or Chrissy knew about it?' She stroked Rebus. 'It's Finn's day off today and so I'm going to pop round to the house.'

'Hopefully, the response will provide a phone number. Then we can ring and ask some proper questions.'

Ellie's brain was shifting up the gears. 'That's a lot of people to speak to.'

Sylvia stood up. 'I suggest we sit down with some breakfast and divide it up. Most importantly, you must not go anywhere alone until we find out who sent you the death threat.'

Ellie nodded. 'I'm not going to. Don't worry.'

'Did you get any sleep?' Sylvia asked Ellie kindly.

'A bit.' She stroked Rebus' ears. 'Thank you. For last night, for everything really. You must have got to bed late. I don't know what time you came up but I'm pretty sure you were downstairs well after Dave left.'

'I couldn't switch off. He was very drunk. It's not like him. But it wasn't just that. It's your death threat, Robert's murder, this new cleaning company.'

Ellie smiled. With her own mother living in France, she appreciated having Sylvia to share with.

'Speaking of Dave... Do you want to talk about him – or not?' Sylvia rubbed her eyes and squinted in the morning light.

'Thanks, no. I was having difficulty trusting him before all this stuff kicked off with Ruby. And that's not necessarily his fault. But now it's a million times more difficult, and it's boring and draining.' She forced a pained smile. 'Anyway – I'll let you get dressed.'

'Ellie, before you go... Generally, I don't repeat things that people tell me. But I'm going to tell you this because I think it's important. Last night, when Dave was here, he said he had messed up.'

'Oh?'

'Uh-huh. Now, I have no idea what he meant because I told him I didn't want to know. But, whatever he's got wrong, he's aware of it. Perhaps you could ask him about it?'

———*ell*———

Half an hour later, Ellie, Sylvia and Zoe were around the kitchen table, eating breakfast. Sylvia had updated her granddaughter on what they'd learnt about BluePrint and about Chrissy.

Zoe had taken over her mum's list. 'So, we've got Chrissy, Tracy, Finn, Pete and Kathy. Who else do we need to speak to?'

'That's it.'

'Kathy's one of my godmothers,' Zoe added. 'I really hope she's not involved.'

'This is the thing. They're all our friends and neighbours.' Ellie was checking the Blix Blitz diary. 'One of your jobs has cancelled, Zoe, so can you come with me, please? Sylvia's using your dad's car.'

'Sure.'

'I'll go to see Chrissy first thing,' Sylvia said.

'Zoe, we can pay a visit to Kathy on the way to Finn's, then Tracy and then Pete at the garden centre.' Ellie's thoughts drifted. 'You know, something else is bugging me and I cannot for the life of me figure out what it is. There's something about Robert's murder that we aren't seeing.'

'Some*thing*? Or some*one*?'

'I don't know.' She paused. 'I keep coming back to Andy because—'

'... he's a bit of a thug?'

'That's what I'm wondering,' Ellie continued.

'Why don't we see the people we've identified and re-group this afternoon?' Sylvia suggested.

'Yes. Let's do that.' Ellie drained her cup. 'It's something to do with what you were saying the other day about why people commit murder. Something about their thinking not making sense to others.'

Chapter 33

9am

As soon as Sylvia arrived at Chrissy's, it was clear she wasn't in. Her car wasn't on the drive and no one answered the door.

How strange. Sylvia had left a message saying she'd be over.

In the garden next door, a dog was barking and a child was giggling. She peered over the wooden fence. Chrissy's little girl, Poppy, was throwing a ball for a chocolate Labrador. Sylvia chuckled at the innocent scene. This must be Coco.

＿＿＿＊＊＿＿＿

'Chrissy left a few hours ago,' Pamela, the neighbour, explained a few minutes later with a warm smile. She fastened the buttons on her mauve cardigan and picked up Poppy's teddy from the stairs. 'My husband and I are retired, so when she asked if we would have Poppy and Coco for the morning we were delighted to help.' A neat bob framed her round face. 'Our son has just moved to Australia, so we don't get to see him – or our grandchildren – much now.'

'That must be nice for all of you. Other than today, have you had her recently?' If Chrissy had gone to the woods on Thursday morning, Sylvia was wondering whether she had taken Poppy with her.

'We had her overnight on Wednesday. Chrissy was going dawn swimming and asked if we would look after Poppy. Had a lovely time, didn't we Nigel? Took her along the River Stour and played Poohsticks.'

Sylvia smiled. 'Did Chrissy say where she was going today?'

'The golf course in Deal. Something about her husband. She brought Poppy and Coco over and off she went.'

Chapter 34

9am

Kieran and Emily were playing in their bedrooms upstairs when Ellie and Zoe arrived at Tracy's house.

Ellie took a seat at Tracy's kitchen table and Zoe followed suit.

'How did you get on with Chrissy yesterday?' Ellie asked. 'Did you manage to get a few things sorted out?' This wasn't really what she wanted to talk about, but she was hoping it would enable her to ask Tracy about Robert's franchise business.

'Not much.' Tracy was still in her pyjamas and dressing gown. 'I think we're still both taking in the shock of it all. Not just Robert's death but finding out about each other.'

'I'm afraid we've discovered a few things about Robert that we need to ask you about,' Ellie said.

'That doesn't sound like it's going to be good news,' Tracy replied. 'What is it?'

Ellie had thought carefully about how to phrase things. 'Did Robert ever tell you what sort of franchises he was selling?' She studied Tracy's face.

Tracy frowned and pursed her lips as though she was trying to think back. 'I don't think so.'

'Are you sure?' Zoe asked.

'I think so. To be honest, I've been so busy, he could have told me and I might not have remembered.' She filled up the kettle and started getting out mugs.

'You see, the reason I'm asking is that I've had a few cleaning customers cancel their contracts with me recently.' Ellie brought up the BluePrint website on her phone.

'Sorry to hear that. But what's that got to do with Robert's franchises?' Tracy got milk out of the fridge.

Ellie let the question hang in the air for a few moments to gauge whether Tracy had a clue about her husband's activities. 'This was what we couldn't figure out for a while too. But, after a bit of digging, we found out that BluePrint, the company that you said your husband worked for, is linked to a national company which offers local cleaning services in a number of areas round here.

They do it via franchises.' Ellie continued to watch Tracy's reactions.

'Are you telling me that Robert has been selling *cleaning franchises*?' Tracy joined them at the table.

'That's how it looks, I'm afraid,' Zoe said.

Ellie held out her phone so Tracy could see the website. 'He sold one which covers the Wootton area, and it has been using some pretty underhand tactics to get my customers to switch to them. Did you know anything about this?'

'No.'

Ellie told Tracy about the leaflets, the company branding, deliberately trying to give the impression that they were Blix Blitz.

As Ellie spoke, a look of pain spread over Tracy's face.

'Oh, Ellie. This is awful. I'm really sorry.' She slouched over the table. 'I had no idea he was selling cleaning franchises. There were many times when Robert would talk about what he was doing, and I didn't listen because I wasn't interested. All I cared about was that he paid his share of the mortgage and the bills and supported Kieran and Emily.' She stood up, walked to the sink and filled a glass with water. 'I'm quite sure if he had mentioned *anything* to do with cleaning, it would have set off alarm bells. I know, just like everyone else does round here, that you run Blix Blitz.'

Ellie listened and she got the impression Tracy was telling the truth.

'If only I'd listened properly. Asked more questions. Perhaps I could've stopped this cleaning franchise thing.'

Chapter 35

9.45am

Ellie clipped Rebus' lead onto his collar. She and Zoe were back from Tracy's and were about to walk over to Finn's house. There were plenty of people around, but Ellie wasn't taking any chances by going on her own.

Normally, when Ellie crossed the green with Rebus, she let him have a good run on the grass. On Saturdays, however, Rebus' freedom had to be constrained to stop him from snaffling a camembert or pack of pâté from the cheese stall at the Saturday market. In addition, the farmer's sheep were in their pen for tomorrow's open day at the windmill.

As they walked, the two of them passed the stall holders, most of whom were from the local villages. They were pottering about, chatting, helping each out with change and covering each other's stalls when they needed the loo.

Many had become friends of Ellie and Dave's over the years.

Each week there was someone new. Today, it was a stall selling delicious-smelling craft beers from Kent. Finn and Charlie would like those. She waved at the woman selling jams and pickles. What was her name? Dave had played darts with her husband. On the wool stall, her friend's daughter was manning things today. They had loaned Ellie needles and patterns when she was pregnant with Simon and couldn't sleep.

Kathy's bakery had their trailer open. They weren't busy.

Ellie spotted Kathy and stopped. 'Morning,' she said. 'Could I ask you a couple of questions about the farm shop? Sally and Tracy have roped us into investigating Robert's death.'

'Sure,' said Kathy, lowering her voice. 'Nick said he'd filled you in.' She emptied the espresso container and wiped the metal. 'Do you want a coffee while you're here?'

'No thanks. We've got a list of people to see this morning and final preparations to make for the open day tomorrow.'

'Fire away then.'

'When did you last have any communication with Robert?'

'Let me see. Months ago.'

'Absolutely none since then?'

'None. After what he did to Nick, Pete and me, I vowed I'd never speak to him again.'

'I gather you stopped him in the end. What did you do?'

'All Robert cared about was money, so I took him to court.' She wiped the trailer counter. 'We should've done it sooner. Before things got out of hand.'

'It's village life, isn't it? We all know each other and – with the exceptions of pond-life like Robert – none of us wants to rock the boat. I've found it tough, having to ask friends personal questions about what they've been doing and why.'

'Any idea who's responsible?'

'Getting closer.'

Ellie said goodbye, and a few minutes later she and Zoe were walking towards the Priest House, where Finn lived. Two roads back from the high street, it was a rambling seventeenth-century stone building, originally part of the old Catholic convent and chapel.

As they approached, Ellie felt her body constricting. The last time she had been here, Andrea, Finn's mother, had just been murdered, and Ellie had found out that Andrea and Dave had briefly had an affair.

Ellie opened the gate – which was no longer creaky – and Rebus towed her up the path to the front door. Zoe followed behind.

Finn had kept the paint colour his mother had chosen and given it a fresh coat. Beside the door, a young wisteria plant was throwing out new shoots in a beautiful black pot. Ellie caught sight of a slate plaque which Finn had secured to the container.

For Mum. May your light shine forever.

Zoe caught up.

Ellie heard purring and Andrea's cat lolloped towards them. 'Hey, Mouse.' She reached for the doorbell and bent down to stroke the cat.

Rebus started squealing and squirming at the thought of seeing Finn.

A few moments later, Finn opened the door. 'Morning.' He gave Zoe a kiss and crouched down and fussed over Rebus, unclipping his lead. 'You don't need to ring the bell, Ellie. Just knock and walk in.' He stood back to allow them to enter.

'You've made the house look gorgeous,' Ellie said. 'Lovely touch with the wisteria.'

'Thank you. Liam got it from the garden centre. The cobbler in the village engraved the plaque for me.'

The three of them shuffled along the hall into the kitchen, chatting, Rebus bounding ahead.

'Did you get a reply to the e-mail you sent to BluePrint?'

'This morning, yeah.'

Zoe told him about Sylvia's late-night discovery.

'Selling cleaning franchises? So he put Nick and Pete's businesses under strain when he was at the farm shop—?'

'... *and* the bakery.' Zoe told him about Kathy.

'What a creep. And now he's doing similar with Blix Blitz?'

Zoe was playing with Mouse.

'So it seems.' Ellie looked around. It was a large space, made of two rooms knocked through.

Tangles of charging leads.

A laptop, baseball cap, bottle of energy drink.

Beard oil and a Bluebell Railway mug.

Running shoes and protein supplements.

The open plan kitchen was still Andrea's in terms of the base furniture. Much was the same as when Ellie was last here. The oak table and chairs. Butler-style sink. Cream cabinets. Pans hanging from elegant wrought iron hooks in the ceiling. But now it was the home of young men. For a moment, the items which were scattered about reminded her of Simon's room at the windmill, the room Sylvia had now taken over.

Next to the energy drink Ellie spotted a shield with straps like the one Rebus had found in the woods the day before with Sally. 'What's that?' It was made of brown leather and looked new.

'An arm guard. For archery. It's Charlie's.' Finn slipped his phone out of his pocket. 'Here. It's the reply from Wootton Cleaners. See what you think.' He swiped the screen and passed it to Ellie, open at his e-mail.

Eager for information on who was targeting her customers, Ellie's attention drifted from the arm guard. She scanned the message, then read bits aloud. 'We value your inquiry... local Wootton company... price restructure... rewarding *your* loyalty...the people you know and trust.' She looked up. 'Crikey.'

'They're *definitely* trying to pretend they are Blix Blitz,' Zoe said, 'and *definitely* trying to poach our customers.

Ellie continued reading. 'A phone number. That's handy.' She photographed the message.

'Whose is the beard oil?' Zoe asked.

Ellie caught her daughter's tone and stopped reading.

Neither Finn nor Charlie had beards.

'Liam's,' Finn replied. 'The Bluebell Railway mug is his too. It's his pride and joy. Had it since he was a kid.' He picked up the faded mug and briefly examined the steam train image on it. 'Liam's going to move in, I think. Although he's a bit worried about his old man.'

'Worried in what way?' Ellie assumed Finn meant that Andy didn't want his son leaving home.

'How his dad will cope.' Finn was looking at Zoe now. 'I was going to check with you, Zo. You're here a lot and I don't want you feeling pushed out—'

'I don't mind. I'd much prefer to live with Mum and Gran at the windmill. I wouldn't fancy sharing with three smelly guys anyway.'

'Can't imagine why, can you?' Finn snorted and filled the kettle. 'Tea?'

'No, thanks.' Zoe replied quickly, repeating her mother's expression from earlier with Kathy. 'We've got lots of people to see this morning.'

Ellie put her arm out to Zoe. She could see her daughter was upset and wasn't sure whether to wade into Finn's news about Liam moving in. Probably best to leave it to them or speak to Zoe about it later. She was trying to think how she could ask about Liam without being too blunt. 'It's lovely that you three boys get on so well together. How is Liam coping with his stepdad's death?'

'OK, I think,' Finn replied. 'Nothing much seems to have changed. Liam is just as laid back as usual.'

'Well, that's good.'

'He's never liked Robert and has always been close to Andy and his mum. He doesn't talk about his feelings much, so I don't really know the details. To be honest, you're probably better off asking him about it.' He paused. 'Or... Zo? You know Liam quite well. You guys were an item for a while at school.'

'Really?' Ellie said. 'I didn't know that.'

'Didn't last long,' Zoe replied. She opened the French windows and wandered into the garden.

'I need to grab a shower,' Finn said. 'I'm meeting Bob. The timber has arrived for the stocks for the open day tomorrow. We're going to build them this morning.'

Ellie was enjoying seeing how much more settled Finn was becoming. Starting as Bob's tree surgeon apprentice had been a good move. 'It's going to be lots of fun,' she said. 'Kathy and her sister are doing traditional basket weaving this year and the farmer's doing lamb feeding.'

'I'm looking forward to it. Are you OK down here while I get dressed?' Finn glanced over at the French windows as though he wasn't sure whether to go and speak to Zoe.

'Sure. We'll be off in a minute. We can let ourselves out.'

'Have a look round if you fancy. I haven't changed much. Just a bit of TLC for the things that weren't working.' He gave a sad smile. 'I like it the way Mum had it.'

'Before you go – the arm guard.' She told Finn about the one in the woods.

'Charlie's often in there,' he replied. 'When no-one's around, he uses the trees for target practice. Probably dropped that one ages ago. You know what Rebus is like, digging up all kinds of stuff. Some other dog's probably run off with it by now.'

Ellie felt conflicted. Should she tell Dave about the arm guard? Wouldn't that be dobbing Charlie in? This sleuthing business was turning into a nightmare.

Ellie was about to follow Zoe out into the garden when she heard crying up at Andrea's old wooden arbour by the hedge. She scuttled over and sat down on the bench next to Zoe. 'Oh, sweetie. Are you upset about Liam moving in?'

Zoe nodded, sniffing.

On top of everything, it looked like there were changes ahead for Zoe and Finn too.

Chapter 36

10.30am

On her way back to Deal, Sylvia stopped off at St Nicholas' church in Harbledown, where Robert and Chrissy had got married. She wanted to know what Robert had told the vicar about his marital status.

Sylvia stopped the car just outside the church. It was a rag-stone and flint building in the corner of a small graveyard. The large, brown, wooden door was shut and there was no sign of anyone about.

Hopefully, the vicar might be inside.

She parked the car, walked up the path and tried the door, but it was locked. Not her day for finding people in. Then she saw a folded piece of A4 paper pinned to the door frame. She removed the pin and unfolded it.

'Won't be long. Nipped back to the vicarage to get some toilet paper. Reverend Jackson.'

She laughed.

He couldn't have gone far.

She wrote a quick reply on the bottom.

'Dear Rev Jackson,

Please come to Lower Wootton Garden Centre on Appledown Road urgently today, Saturday. It's to do with the murder of one of your parishioners.

Regards, Sylvia Blix.'

She added her mobile number.

Chapter 37

10.45am

Nausea was pulling at Ellie's stomach as she drove into the garden centre with Zoe. She was dreading getting confirmation from Pete that the sabotaged pipe might have given him a motive for wishing Robert harm. Thank goodness she had Zoe with her.

Liam was out front, using a forklift to unload pallets of stones, compost and bark.

Ellie got out of the car and waved at him.

'I'm going to have a quick word with Liam, Mum,' Zoe said. 'I'll catch you up.'

'OK, lovey.' Ellie typed out a text to Dave, telling him about Charlie's arm guard in Appledown Woods. She tucked her phone back in her pocket and went inside to find Pete, who was in the café, serving in a blue and white apron.

As Ellie walked over, he was cutting a Victoria sponge into slices.

Pete took a deep breath when he saw Ellie and for a moment her instinct was to walk back out. He glanced from one side of the café to another and wiped his hands on a tea towel. Then he came round from behind the counter and walked towards her. 'Shall we go outside? It's a bit more private.'

'Sure.' Ellie looked about for Zoe, but she still hadn't come in. 'Sally told me about the pipe and that you suspect Robert deliberately damaged it. Is that right?' She followed him towards the back doors which opened out.

He nodded. 'Unfortunately.'

Ellie's phone started vibrating in her pocket.

'Do you want to explain why? Because if he did damage it, I'm wondering if... if—'

'... if I might've wished him harm?'

'Yes.' Ellie thought about Sylvia's comment that people's actions often don't make sense to others because they are being viewed from their own perspective.

'I haven't told the police yet because I know it incriminates me but I'm obviously going to have to. You might as well know first, though, given you're here, and given it relates to *you*.'

'Me?' What the heck was he about to say?

'Plus, I knew you weren't going to give up asking.' He paused and pointed to a cluster of tall trees. 'Let's go right to the back, if you don't mind.'

Ellie thought about the note on her windscreen.

'*You need to learn when to quit. It would be awful if you ended up like Robert Seale.*'

Her phone stopped buzzing and she shivered.

She wished Zoe had come in with her.

Ellie came to a halt short of the trees. 'Here is fine.' They were in the sightline of the shop. 'What is this about? You mentioned me.'

'Yes. After the business with the farm shop, Nick, Kathy and I all had Robert under close scrutiny. It came to our attention recently that he was selling cleaning franchises.'

'You knew? How did you find *that* out?'

'It was Kathy who first twigged. You know what she's like. Never misses a trick. Like you, she never quits.' He was looking at her with a strange expression.

Ellie held her breath.

'To start with, we didn't care what he was doing, as long as it had nothing to do with the village. But Kathy was angry about the way Robert ripped off so many of us and she refused to let it happen to anyone else. And then she got suspicious. She paid a private investigator to look into BluePrint Franchises.'

'That was sharp of her.'

'When she got his report back, it stated that one of the cleaning franchises that Robert had sold was not just operating round here, it was *deliberately* undercutting your prices and trying to steal your business.'

Ellie gasped. 'Why didn't you tell me?'

'We all knew what an awful year you'd had.'

Her phone started vibrating again.

'The separation from Dave,' Pete continued. 'Andrea's murder. Having to cover Zoe's cleaning jobs while she was ill. We all saw how much you were struggling.'

'Oh, Pete.' Her pulse was slowing.

'When you hired new staff, we were all relieved. Then Robert's franchisee started poaching your customers.'

'What did you do?'

'Nick and I told Kathy to stay out of it this time. We arranged to meet Robert first thing on Thursday morning. We wanted an end to it. He said he was working in Surrey and that was the only time he could make. He wanted to meet somewhere private, away from our houses, and suggested Rattling Folly in the woods.'

'What were you hoping to achieve by meeting him?'

'We wanted him to refund the money to the people who bought the cleaning franchise that covers your area and cancel their contract.'

Ellie was absorbing the news. 'Did anyone else know that he was selling cleaning franchises apart from you, Kathy and Nick?'

'Not as far as we know.'

'What time did you arrange to meet him?'

'6am. That suited both Nick and I as we both get up early.'

'What happened?'

'At first, he agreed to the meeting reluctantly, but when we told him that we knew what he was up to, he was extremely keen to talk to us and keep us quiet. But he didn't turn up.'

'And what? Did you both go home?'

'Pretty much. We rang his mobile, but he didn't answer so we went to the café in the village and had a quick breakfast. We tried his phone again, still no answer, so I came here to the garden centre and Nick went to the shop in the high street.'

'You didn't look for him?'

'No. He was busy so we had no reason to think he would be anywhere else than where he had arranged to meet us.'

'How odd.'

'He confirmed he would be there – and wasn't.'

'Did you see anything strange in the woods? Was anyone else there?'

'Not that we saw.' He placed his hand on his chest. 'It was just us and the wildlife.'

'You didn't walk to the stream, looking for him, or anything like that?'

'Absolutely not. We weren't there for a jolly. We went to the folly to meet him. That was it. He didn't show up and we left.'

'Fair enough.' Robert was probably already dead by the time Nick and Pete arrived. 'When did you discover the water leak?'

'After breakfast, when I got to the garden centre.'

'When do you think he damaged the pipe?'

'I don't know for certain, but I think it was sometime from Wednesday night onwards. My guess is probably in the early hours of Thursday morning.'

That would tally with him being killed at 5am.

'The insurance company investigators might have a better idea, or the police,' Pete added.

'Why didn't the pipe burst immediately?' Ellie didn't know very much about plumbing.

'Robert will have known exactly what to do to create whatever effect he wanted. Presumably, that was to flood my shop while we were at the wedding. It may be that the leak started before I got here on Thursday morning and it was only a very minor trickle then.'

'... which increased slowly?'

'That's my guess.'

'How do you know it was sabotaged?'

'The pipe had a small cut in it.'

'The insurance company will be able to establish whether the cut was deliberate. But why would Robert want to create a flood in the garden centre?'

'He was a very vindictive man, and he was angry that we had called him out on his behaviour at the farm shop and had rumbled his new venture with this franchising business.'

'I know you said you're going to tell the police, but this is urgent now. They'll understand what happened.' Ellie was trying to decide what to do next. She no longer thought Pete might have left the death threat on her car, but she wasn't sure whether she believed him about meeting Robert in the woods.

Was it possible that he and Nick had lured Robert there... and killed him?

Ellie was about to leave when Zoe came charging over. 'Gran called. Chrissy's not at home. She's gone to Deal.'

Chapter 38

11.30am

S ylvia had never been to an archery range before and was surprised by how busy it was. The reception area was full of people of all ages, milling about and buying equipment. In the café, families were enjoying snacks.

She walked up to the desk. 'I'm Sylvia Blix. I rang earlier to ask whether Mr Morris was a regular member here. Could I just check that we're both talking about the same person?'

The receptionist nodded. 'We have his membership photo, but I'm not allowed to show you.' She used her biro to point at a laminated sign. 'Centre rules, I'm afraid.'

'No problem.' Sylvia had the photos Ellie had sent. She swiped her phone into life and showed the receptionist an image. 'Are we talking about this person...?' She showed another photograph, '... or this one?'

'They're both members. But the second one comes here every week, like clockwork. Really good shot too.'

Chapter 39

11.45am

E llie was driving when Zoe's phone pinged with a Google alert.

Zoe swiped her phone and opened her e-mail. The link took her to an article on the *Wootton Gazette* website. The headline said: SECOND MURDER.

'There's been another death,' Zoe told Ellie.

'Oh no. What does it say?'

Zoe read aloud. '*Woman found dead on golf course.*'

'Chrissy,' they chimed.

'Seems most likely,' Ellie said. 'Read the rest, can you, lovey?'

Zoe began: '*Breaking news. A local woman has been found dead in a World War Two Pillbox on Deal golf course. A dog walker found the woman face down. At present, it is not known whether this death and Robert*

Seale's are connected. We are unable to name the victim at this time.'

Zoe dialled Sylvia's number.

Her voicemail clicked in.

'Gran, if you haven't seen yet, there's been another murder. On the golf course. It's on the Wootton Gazette's website. We're heading over there now. Shall we meet you there?'

Chapter 40

12pm

'I know where the Pillbox is,' Ellie told Zoe. 'We can get to it if we drive along the road past the Clubhouse towards Sandwich Bay.'

Zoe was scrolling on her phone, checking news websites and social media.

Ellie rammed the jeep into gear and sped off along the sea front, past all the detached houses with their posh verandas and turret rooms. She accelerated along Links Road, turning into the Golf Club car park and driving into a space round the back.

She switched off the engine, grabbed her bag and jumped out.

From the car park, the two of them ran along the road and then onto the footpath which would take them to the Pillbox. Within moments they saw the cordon. Marked police cars blocked off the road and blue lights flashed in the open sky. A white tent stood on the hill by the Pillbox.

Zoe slowed. 'Mum, this is awful.'

'I know. Do you want to stay in the car? I can go and meet your gran.'

Zoe shook her head.

Ellie spotted Sylvia sitting on a large wooden post.

'The *Gazette* article still isn't confirming that it's Chrissy but I'm sure it is,' Zoe said.

'I bet the police had a go at Katie Douglas for releasing Robert's name the other day. It won't stop her for long, though. She'll do it again, just maybe not on this...' Ellie stopped speaking as she caught sight of Dave, talking to the white-suited crime scene investigators.

'Ruby's on duty, in case you haven't seen,' Zoe told her mum.

Sylvia met the two of them. 'He's in a foul mood.' She gestured to Dave. 'Hung over, I expect. Already bitten my head off for being too close to the cordon.'

Dave must've heard their voices as he looked up from his clipboard and saw Ellie.

Her stomach glugged and then she got a flutter of butterflies.

Even from a distance she saw Dave's face tighten. He said something to his colleagues and strode towards them.

'Oh God,' Zoe said. 'He really doesn't look happy.'

Ellie ignored his approach and turned to Zoe and Sylvia. 'This changes *everything*,' she told them.

'It really does,' Sylvia agreed. 'I had Chrissy pegged as our main suspect.'

'The two murders have different *modus operandi*,' Zoe said. 'Could it be a different killer?'

'That's a good question.' A thought occurred to Ellie. 'Let's consider who might want Robert *and* Chrissy dead.'

'Robert had annoyed so many people, it was a large pool,' Sylvia replied. 'But who would want Chrissy out of the way? Who round here even knew about her?'

'Theoretically,' said Ellie, 'only Robert, and he's dead. Then there's Tracy and us.'

'Does that mean Tracy killed Robert and Chrissy?' Zoe nudged her mum. 'Dad incoming.'

'It's possible. Unless someone *else* knew about Chrissy and Robert's relationship. They could have killed her.'

'What about Andy Morris?' Sylvia replied. 'He could conceivably want them both gone.'

Ellie was racking her brain for ideas. Ever since Pete had told her about Robert sabotaging the pipe, his suspicious behaviour made sense. But what motive could he have for wanting to kill Chrissy? If they were looking for one killer, Pete didn't fit the bill.

'Ellie.' Dave's voice was so quiet she didn't hear him at first. He wasn't a fan of stubble but hadn't shaved. His eyes were bloodshot and had dark circles underneath. A long, thin scratch stretched across his face.

'Your girlfriend do that?' Ellie pointed to his cheek and then over at Ruby, who was unloading equipment from a vehicle.

'She is *not* my girlfriend.' His words were clipped, his shoulders tense.

'Dad, your face.' Zoe was at his side. 'What happened?'

'If you must know, I fell in a bush on my way home last night.' He spoke quietly. 'Trying to avoid the sheep pen.'

'Oh *dear,*' Ellie said. 'That *was* careless. The pen's only been there every spring for the last ten years.'

'*Dad.*' Zoe did not sound impressed.

'Thank you. That's very helpful. But you go ahead. Have a good laugh. It's extremely sore.' He dabbed at his cheek, giving a wince.

Zoe gave him an affectionate shove.

He shifted tone. 'I couldn't help hearing your conversation as I came over. Please tell me that all three of you are not here, *sleuthing* again?'

'Nope,' Ellie replied. 'We are about to head off.'

'Where are you going?'

'It's none of your business.'

He sighed loudly. 'Thank you. I'll remember that. Can you three, please, stay together? We haven't got an ID yet on the prints on your death threat note.'

'Righto, Inspector,' Ellie said, knowing she was being a bit childish.

Dave strode back over to join his colleagues.

'He isn't happy,' Zoe said, staring after her dad. 'Something's definitely up with him.'

'Where were we?' Ellie asked.

'... discussing who might want Chrissy dead,' Sylvia replied.

'Oh, yes. Tracy. She has clearly been fed up with Robert for a long time. Except she had the opportunity to separate from him and get a divorce, and she said no.'

'It's what Gran was talking about,' Zoe said, returning her attention to her mum and grandmother. 'Robert didn't want him and Tracy to separate. Maybe he was better off financially if he stayed married to Tracy? Maybe she got to the end of her tether, and decided to take matters into her own hands?' She was twiddling her plaits.

'Or when she found out about Chrissy, that could have tipped her over the edge and she decided to bump them *both* off,' Sylvia added. 'We know she's a darn good archer. Nick confirmed it.'

'Uh-oh, look who's just arrived.' Zoe had noticed first. 'That's not going to go down well with Dad.'

Katie Douglas was walking towards them in a cream leather jacket and black jeans, her red top knot bright in the spring light.

'Come on,' Ellie said. 'We aren't going to find anything here. And it would be best to leave Dave in peace. Shall we all head over to the garden centre? I want to ask Liam about his father.'

Chapter 41

12.30pm

Ellie, Sylvia and Zoe were unusually quiet as they walked back to fetch the jeep. There had been another death, and there was another grieving family.

They left the Audi at the Golf Club and were soon driving towards the garden centre.

'I can't get over Dad falling in a bush.' Zoe was the first to speak.

'There's definitely something bothering him,' Sylvia replied. 'My son's no saint. And he likes a drink. But I don't think I can remember him doing anything like that.'

'Speaking of things that have been bothering people, Zoe, when I asked you about Liam earlier, you wandered off. I appreciate that might have been about Finn and—'

'It was ages ago,' Zoe replied. 'At school. Didn't really work so we knocked it on the head.'

'What didn't work?'

'I'm not sure I can pinpoint it. He was lovely. He *is* lovely. The most placid, chilled out person you could meet most of the time, but occasionally something would set him off and he would get possessive and angry. It made me a bit scared of him.'

'I'm glad you had the sense to walk away then. Did he say much about his stepdad?'

'He hated him.' That confirmed what Finn had said.

Their conversation drifted to Simon and Jen's engagement and before they knew it, they'd arrived at the garden centre.

Liam was out the front, watering trolleys of plants with a hose.

'Wonder if he's heard about Chrissy's murder?' Zoe asked.

'You know what the village grapevine is like,' Sylvia said. 'And he's probably seen the *Gazette* article.'

Zoe's question sent ideas clicking into place in Ellie's mind. Realisations poured in. 'Zoe, I need you to make some calls. I know who killed Robert and Chrissy.'

'You're kidding?'

'We need to get everyone here, to the garden centre ASAP. I want you to call Pete. He's probably just inside, but *phone him* rather than go in, please. Tell him it's important and to be discreet, and to go and collect Sally and Tracy immediately and bring them here.'

'OK.'

'Sylvia, can you call Nick at the butcher's? Ask him to collect Andy Morris from the gym on the main road by Priory Park and to come straight here too.'

'Sure.'

'I'll call Finn and Dave. Then I'm going to go over and chat to Liam about his father.'

As Ellie got out of the jeep, she heard Zoe and Sylvia start making calls. She walked over to Liam. 'Hi. I was at Finn's house earlier. Saw the lovely wisteria that you gave him. That was a kind gesture.'

He shrugged. 'Oh, you know. He's a good mate.'

'Can I ask you about your stepfather? I know you've said that you got on with him OK... but did you really?'

It had been niggling away at the back of her mind that Liam always said he and Robert got on "OK". But Finn had said Liam hated Robert. That was a big difference. And Zoe had just confirmed what Finn said.

Liam stared at Ellie, as though he was not just deciding what to say but searching within himself for how he felt. 'I hated him,' he said quietly. 'I absolutely hated him.' His voice was more forceful now. 'He broke up my parents' marriage. He told Mum he would look after her, be kind to her, and he wasn't. He made her miserable. My dad wasn't perfect but there was absolutely no reason for them to split up. Dad loved Mum. And Robert Seale took her away from him.'

——ele——

Twenty minutes later, Pete had collected Sally and Tracy and had closed the garden centre back doors. Zoe and Dave had gone to pick up Finn and were on their way back. Ellie and Sylvia were assembling everyone in the café.

Andy Morris had reluctantly agreed to leave work but had refused to get into Nick's car. He, therefore, arrived in his pickup, looking agitated.

'What's going on?' Andy was already on the offensive. 'What's this all about?'

Ellie began addressing the group. 'There have been two deaths in and around the village, both of them murders, and we thought we would have a little *discussion*. Sally and Tracy asked Sylvia, Zoe and me to investigate.'

Sally joined her sister and linked arms.

'It's been an extremely complicated case,' Ellie continued, 'and has involved a number of people in the village, my family and me. Which is why I've been happy to help.'

'Hear, hear.' Sylvia stood side by side with Ellie.

'Initially, when Zoe and I found Robert dead in the woods, there were so many people he had fallen out with, all people who live in the village. It hasn't been easy or pleasant asking you personal and difficult questions. Lots of you had motives. Pete, Robert owed you money, but your behaviour has been extremely odd.'

'He certainly did. And that was just half of it.'

'Nick, your situation was similar.'

'Yes, just as the garden centre suffered from Robert breaking the gentlemen's agreement with Brian and Lily over the farm shop, my butcher's suffered too.'

A clattering at the front of the shop signalled the arrival of Dave, Zoe and Finn.

Zoe ran over to her mum.

'Several other businesses in the village suffered at his hands too,' Nick continued. 'I could quite cheerfully have throttled the scheming so-and-so but I didn't. I would like to know who did though.'

'So would I,' Dave announced. 'Given that we are still ploughing through CCTV and comms data.' He stood to one side of the café, presumably allowing her to get on with whatever she had planned.

Sylvia took over. 'In amongst all this, Ellie has had her business targeted and she has received a death threat. Hard to believe in our friendly and safe community.'

'Very sad, I'm sure, but what's all that got to do with Robert's murder?' Andy demanded.

Sylvia tutted loudly and shot him a disapproving look.

Ellie ignored his question. 'One of the things that we can't escape from when we live in a village like ours is that we are all affected by each other's lives. And although it is a cliché, we often really don't know what is going on behind closed doors.'

'Very true,' said Nick.

'Some of you are probably wondering who Chrissy is.' Ellie glanced at Pete and Nick and Andy. Did any of them have an inkling? 'You all know, of course, that Tracy and Andy got divorced and that Tracy married Robert.'

'Is there a point to all this?' shouted Andy. 'Because, if you've just got us here to rake up the past, I've got a client waiting to finish his bench presses at the gym.'

Ellie continued. 'What many of you don't know is that Robert also had a *wife and daughter* in Canterbury.'

There was a collective intake of breath.

Ellie cast about the warehouse, checking facial expressions and reactions. 'Robert and Chrissy got married in Harbledown five years ago and they have a little girl called Poppy.'

'You're kidding?' Nick said loudly.

'I wish I was.'

'What an absolute swine,' Nick added. 'So, he breaks up Tracy and Andy's marriage, marries Tracy and then goes off and marries another woman at the same time?'

'That's about it,' Tracy said. 'Not forgetting poor Poppy, who is completely innocent in all of this. It was certainly a surprise to me, and from what I can gather, it was also a surprise to Chrissy. So, when we thought he was away on business, he was not. He was shuttling over to his other family for a few days with them before coming back. Which he has – unbelievably – done on play and repeat for the last few years.'

'And you didn't know?' Andy barked at Tracy.

'I've just said I didn't.'

'He's lucky I didn't get my hands on him.'

Dave's attention was immediately on Andy.

'This is where we come to the "means".' Ellie looked at Sylvia. 'Nobody got their "hands" on either Robert or Chrissy. I'll come onto Chrissy in a moment, but Robert was shot by an arrow which was stolen from the Matthews' house last week. And this is where it got even more complex.'

Sylvia took over. 'Now, you might think, like I did, that the number of villagers with archery as a hobby is very low. However, not only do we have a number of early risers in Lower Wootton, we also have several bow and arrow enthusiasts, partly as a result of your club, Nick. Who wants to raise their hand if archery is something they have done or still do?'

Andy groaned loudly.

Ellie surveyed the café area.

'*Raise our hand?* Are we back at school?' Andy sneered.

'Something like that,' Sylvia replied. 'Put your hand up then, Andy.'

'You what, doll?'

'Sandwich Archery Range say they see you regularly.'

'It's hardly a secret, Andy,' said Nick. 'Although why you might want to keep it as one, I have no idea. Charlie and I have competed against you several times. As has another person in this room.' He turned and faced Tracy.

'Oops. Hand up, Trace,' Andy jeered. 'I think you've been busted too.'

Dave was following the back-and-forth.

'I have done archery, yes,' Tracy said. 'Not recently though. I've been too busy trying to look after my kids, do a job and keep a home running.'

'Anyone else?' Ellie peered at her daughter and then her mother-in-law. 'No. We haven't either.' She looked over at Liam. 'How about you?'

'Yeah. I do a bit of archery. I go with Dad sometimes. Nothing wrong with that, is there?'

It was the first time Ellie had heard Liam sound even slightly irritable. Previously, when she'd spoken to him, he'd been warm and polite.

Ellie was tempted to say, 'Only if someone has been killed with a bow and arrow' but she figured that was self-evident. 'We then realised, as I'm sure you can guess, that we were looking for someone with not just archery skill but also a compelling reason for wanting Robert and Chrissy out of the way.' She fixed her gaze on Andy.

'What are you staring at me for?' he said immediately. 'I haven't touched either of them.' He swivelled his attention from Ellie to Dave. 'This is the first I've heard of Chrissy. Didn't know she existed, only just learnt she's been killed, and had no idea – until you just mentioned it – that she was Robert's other wife.'

'Are you sure about that?' Tracy's eyes flashed and saliva spattered from her mouth as she spoke. 'You're constantly checking up on me, checking up on Liam. Are you telling me you had no idea that Robert had this other family?'

'Yeah, I *am* telling you that,' he snarled back. 'If you think you know otherwise, where's your proof?'

'I don't have any,' Tracy replied. 'I'm just asking because it wouldn't surprise me.'

'I could ask the same of you. Did you *really* not know that your husband had another family?'

'I definitely did not. But someone obviously did. Ellie, you must know who, otherwise you wouldn't have got us all together here.'

'Mum?' Zoe was staring at Ellie.

'Actually, it all became more obvious after Chrissy was killed.' She surveyed the room. 'I mentioned that I, too, have got caught up in this case. Robert sold a cleaning franchise to someone who has been poaching my customers. Pete and Nick found out about it and were in the woods the morning that Robert was killed. They'd arranged to meet Robert to confront him about the sale of the franchise.'

'Good grief,' Dave muttered. 'I'll need to speak to both of you – again.'

'And it was something Sylvia said that got the pennies dropping,' Ellie added. 'She said people sometimes commit murder to achieve a goal when they've tried all the other stuff and run out of options.'

She looked at Liam, whose face was expressionless.

'You see, I've been trying to figure out why you didn't seem to mind about your parents' divorce. Why you didn't seem to mind about your mum marrying Robert. Why you said you got on OK with him. Everyone says how placid you are. How nothing bothers you. And it made me realise that simply cannot be true.'

Sylvia spoke up. 'It's not natural to feel nothing when our parents split up. Usually when children claim that *this* is how they feel, it's an indicator of denial.'

Liam was shaking his head and fidgeting.

'A few things gave it away,' Ellie said. 'It's obvious, for example, that you care deeply about both your mother and your father.'

He raised his head.

'Your treasured mug from the Bluebell Railway. Was that from a family day out with your mum and dad?'

'It was such a perfect day. Mum loves steam trains.' Liam's voice warmed as he spoke. 'Dad bought us lemonade lollies from the kiosk at the station and the guard explained how the piston and cylinder work.'

'It must've been hard for you when they split up.'

'Uh-huh.'

'Perhaps when Tracy married Robert, before things went wrong between them, you worried less about her?'

Ellie asked. 'Was it easier to focus your attention on your dad?'

She didn't want to confront Liam with Finn's words because it would put the two friends in a difficult situation.

'For example, I've been wondering if you worried about your father more than he worried about you.'

'Now you hang on a minute,' Andy boomed. 'That is *not* true.'

Ellie ignored him. She was more concerned about not quoting her daughter's words either. 'An old friend of yours from school told us that you were generally pretty placid until you really, really weren't. They said your mildness dissolved into anger and possessiveness when you were worried the person was going to leave you.'

She paused to check how her words were landing. 'The clincher though came via my cleaner's eagle eye. At Finn's house, I saw your beard oil. Next to it was a brown, leather arm guard.'

Liam's face fell.

'Finn told us the arm guard was Charlie's. But it's not. It's yours, isn't it?' Ellie was counting on Liam not wanting to frame his friend.

He nodded.

'In Appledown Woods the other day, I saw an identical one, although more well-worn. That's yours too, isn't it? Did you drop it when you were there on Thursday?'

Liam was silent.

'Liam? A lot of people care about you, and it might not seem like it right now, but it is possible to get help with these feelings.'

Liam sniffed and wiped his cheek. 'I had to watch Robert bully Mum.' His voice was a whisper. 'Watch him undermine her and criticise her. To start with, maybe he loved her, I don't know. But, whatever he felt, it quickly changed, and I couldn't stand his cruelty towards her. What made it worse was that Dad adored Mum. And that man, *Robert*, he split them up for no good reason at all.' He looked over at Andy, whose face was reddening. 'He split them up, and then decided that he didn't want Mum after all.' He was swallowing hard. 'That was bad enough. But the last straw was him starting an affair with another woman, getting married and having another family. I will never forgive him for that.' He looked around the room at the faces in front of him.

Dave had crept forward and was closer to Ellie. Zoe was twiddling her hair.

'It wasn't hard to find out,' Liam continued. 'I very quickly suspected he was cheating on Mum, so I followed him a few times and ended up in Canterbury.' He wiped his nose on his sleeve. 'To make matters worse, when Mum told him she wanted a divorce, he piled on all the guilt, all the emotional blackmail and she gave in.' He glanced at Tracy, eyes brimming with tears. 'But he lied. He didn't want another chance. He didn't want to make things right. He just didn't want to have to pay for his children if they got divorced.' He kicked at a table leg. 'It was easier for him to get away with paying very little when he and Mum were still married. That's all he wanted. I tried to talk to him about it many times and he laughed at me. He jeered and sneered – just like he did with Mum whenever she challenged him on anything. And I snapped.' Again, he looked at his dad. 'The night before he died, Robert pushed Mum and—'

Tracy said, 'Liam, don't—'

'No, Mum. People need to know what he was like.' He was picking at the skin round his fingers. 'Robert pushed her, and she fell and banged her head on the coffee table. And I knew, I *knew* that if I didn't do something, the next time she might not be so lucky. So, I arranged to meet him in the woods early on Thursday morning and I gave him an ultimatum. Either he granted Mum a divorce or I'd tell the police about his violence. He said a divorce was out of the question and told me I didn't have the guts to go to the police. He laughed about it as though it was funny. Said that how he treated Mum was none of my business. Called her names, and I saw red. I waited until he walked away from me. I fired an arrow into his back and left him to bleed to death in the woods.'

Tracy let out a sob.

Ellie went over and gathered her up in a hug. 'What about Chrissy?' she asked Liam.

'Initially I wondered if I should have had more sympathy or more patience with her,' Liam replied, 'but I didn't. I quickly discovered that she didn't care about Mum either. And she didn't care about Kieran and Emily. She just wanted to get as much for herself as she could, and she didn't give a hoot what happened to his other family. It made me furious. It seemed so unfair and selfish.'

'Did Chrissy know about your mum?'

'Oh, yes. Although I only found this out this morning. She knew their marriage would be void. That she and Poppy had no legal rights. So, she got Robert to put some of his assets in her name.'

Tracy gasped.

'Did she tell him she knew about the bigamy?'

'Yes. And she was clever. She was protecting her own interests but told Robert it would prevent Mum from getting her hands on his money.'

Sylvia sucked in a deep breath. 'Whereas it was her insurance policy.'

'So, you killed Chrissy too?' Ellie swallowed as she thought about Kieran, Emily and Poppy.

'I arranged to meet her for a walk on the golf course so I could find out what her intentions were now that Robert was dead. She had no legal rights but I wanted to know if she was planning to make things difficult for Mum.'

'What did she say?' Tracy's voice was quiet.

'She admitted she'd known about the bigamy, and said you only had yourself to blame. According to her, it wouldn't have happened if you had divorced Robert–'

'It was *my* fault? That's out of order. He wouldn't divorce *me*.'

'He'd told her it was the other way round. Anyway, she started on at me. Said Dad had left *you* because of me. That *you* didn't care about me either. She called me all sorts of names. Useless, worthless, selfish… all I could feel was rage.'

'Oh, Liam. Sweetheart.' Tracy's words came out on a sob. 'None of that is true.'

'What did you do?' Ellie asked.

'All I could feel was rage. I lured her into the old Pillbox and strangled her.'

'Did you break into the Matthews' and steal archery equipment from them?'

Liam nodded. 'I have my own bow and arrow so I was hoping it would divert attention away from me.'

'You must've been pretty sure your conversation with your stepdad wasn't going to go well then?'

It was desperately sad. Liam had felt he had no other options. And, if Robert hadn't broken up Tracy and Andy's marriage, perhaps none of it would have happened.

'What about my phone?' Tracy asked. 'Why did you leave it by the body for the police to find?'

'I'm really sorry, Mum. I didn't mean to. You dropped it on the drive. I had it to give to you and it slipped out of my jeans pocket. By the time I realised, it was too late to go back for it.'

The door burst open and a tall man loped through the shop towards the café. He had round glasses and wore a long black vicar's cassock, surplice and dog collar. 'I got a message and came as quickly as I could.' He surveyed the group. 'Which of you is Sylvia Blix?'

'Me.' Sylvia stepped forward.

'I'm Reverend Jackson, the vicar at St Nicholas' in Harbledown. You said something about a murder.'

'Thanks so much for coming. I stopped off because you married Robert and Chrissy Seale.' She mentioned his recent death.

'I heard about it on the news. Absolutely tragic. Lovely couple.'

'I'm assuming, when you married them, that you didn't know Robert was already married?' Dave asked from the side of the café.

'*Married?*'

'That's correct.'

'Certainly not. He told me he was divorced.'

'Thank you.'

'I wouldn't have married them if I'd known. In the eyes of God, it's a sin to enter into a new marriage while an existing husband or wife is still alive.'

'We assumed that was the case,' Sylvia said. 'Has anything come to light since you married them? Anyone been to see you?'

'If it had, I would have been obliged to declare it but I can honestly say, with my hand on my heart, that it hasn't.' He glanced about. 'Except since you've asked about people coming to see me, I think you ought to know – if you don't already – that I was concerned when Tony here came to see me...' He pointed at Liam.

Tony?

'I... I don't think anyone here is going to be interested in our boring conversation, Vicar,' Liam replied quickly.

'You seemed so angry,' the vicar continued. 'So angry in fact that it frightened me. I felt scared for you and for others. I had no way of tracking you down. Other than knowing your Christian name, I didn't know who you were.'

'Well done, Mum, that was a good shout.' Dave turned back to the vicar. 'Thank you, Reverend, for coming all the way over here. I am Detective Inspector Blix of the Kent Police, and we will definitely need to speak to you.'

Dave faced Liam.

'Was it you who left the note on Ellie's car?'

Liam looked down and nodded. 'I'm really sorry, Mrs Blix. I wanted Robert to die but I didn't want to get caught and as soon as you started investigating, I knew you'd be onto me.'

'And was it you who briefed the *Gazette*?'

He nodded.

'Liam Morris I am arresting you on the suspicion of murder of Robert Seale and Chrissy Seale. You do not have to say anything, but it might harm your defence if you do not mention something which you later rely on in court.'

Tracy let out a sob.

'Anything you do say may be given in evidence.'

Andy Morris crossed the café and went to comfort his ex-wife.

Chapter 42

DAY 4 - Sunday, 8am

S unday was open day at Wootton Windmill.

By the time Ellie got downstairs at 8am, Sylvia had washed the floor, squirted bleach in the loo, and baked a fresh batch of scones. 'You can never have too many cakes,' she announced when she saw Ellie.

Ellie smiled. Having hosted open day at the mill for a decade, she was usually relaxed, but this year she had no idea how they'd manage it. 'Normally,' she told Sylvia, 'I'm the first to show people round the windmill, to hold their dogs and help them take photos. But today I want to go and hide under my duvet with a book.' She shuffled over to the sash window by the front door.

The local farmer was unloading feeding bottles for the lambs in the pen. In the front seat of his Land Rover, a black and white collie watched everything.

'I hope we are doing the right thing,' she said. With Robert's and Chrissy's deaths, and Liam's arrest, they hadn't been sure whether to cancel the event.

'People travel to the village from miles around. We would never have got word out.'

There was a knock at the door.

When Ellie opened it, Dave and Ruby were standing there. 'Oh,' she said.

'Oh, to you, too.' Dave's scratch was scabbing over and he'd shaved. 'Ruby has come to speak to you, and I've come to collect Rebus.' He was trying to sound business-like.

'*Collect* him?'

'Zoe asked me to have him at mine while... the... open day... is...' His sentence petered out. 'I think we've been "Zoe-ed".' He rolled his eyes.

Ruby stared at them, confused, not part of the family joke.

'I'll get off in a minute then,' Dave said. 'Be back to help with parking, if you still want me to?'

Ellie shrugged.

'Yes, please,' Sylvia shouted through from the kitchen. 'And don't forget Adrian and Jane's wedding reception this afternoon.'

'I said that without moving my lips,' said Ellie.

'By the way, I'm sorry I missed Simon's engagement.'

'It's him you need to apologise to,' Ellie replied.

'Fair enough. Before I go, Ruby has something to tell you about the night before last.'

'Oh?' Ellie shifted her gaze to Ruby, who shrugged and began shuffling from one foot to the other.

'*Don't you?*' Dave said to her. 'About the wine at my flat.'

Ellie caught the irritation in Dave's voice.

'When I arrived,' Ruby muttered begrudgingly, 'Dave had poured out a glass of wine and nodded off on the sofa. I quickly topped up his glass when he went to let you in. Pretended I was drinking it when you arrived.'

Her news softened the pain in Ellie's solar plexus.

Presumably that was why Dave was so dishevelled.

'Why would you do that?' Ellie peered at Ruby, trying to get a sense of what was motivating her.

'Knew it would wind you up, didn't I?'

Ellie bit back a reply. She felt like screaming at her but there was no point. She would have a chat with her and see if she could get some answers. 'Let's wander,' she said. She wasn't about to invite Ruby into her home, so she grabbed her coat and pulled it on. 'Won't be long,' she shouted to Sylvia, leaving Dave standing on the doorstep.

Once they were on the green, Ellie steered Ruby towards the duck pond. 'Why did you send those messages?'

'I'm sure Dave has told you.'

'I want to hear it from you.'

'He's always been kind to me. I just... I'm sorry. They weren't nice.'

'No. They weren't. Are you going to stop now?'

Ruby shrugged. 'Are you going to file a complaint about me?'

'I haven't decided. What were you doing here the other day?'

'I'd come round the previous day to speak to you and my earring came out when I took my jumper off. When you got home, I was looking for it. I should've said. It would've been much easier.'

'Why didn't you?'

'When you said that Dave loved you, I was jealous and felt like winding you up.'

Ellie took her answer in. 'Whatever you're doing, it needs to stop. Here and now. OK?'

Ruby shrugged again.

'You still haven't told me where we've met.'

'At the bash the lads threw for Dave's fortieth.'

It'd clearly made more of an impression on Ruby than it had on Ellie.

'I need to go. I've got a busy day.'

～ℓℓ～

An hour later, Wootton Windmill was a hive of activity and joy. Ellie and Zoe were on the drive, watching the spectacle. The lawn was strewn with families, couples, scooters, children's drink bottles and stuffed toys.

'Mind your backs,' said Sylvia, as she carried out a warmed baby bottle in one hand and a giant teapot in the other.

Sally wasn't far behind, carrying plates of sandwiches.

'Finn said Gran borrowed the teapot from the scout hall,' Zoe whispered to her mum.

Reverend Jackson was sitting at one of the temporary picnic tables. On the plate in front of him was a pecan brownie and a large slice of Sylvia's Victoria sponge.

Not far from him, Kathy and her daughter were showing people how to weave traditional willow baskets. A selection of their creations was displayed on the table in front of them.

Pennypot Lane was a mass of cars. Dave and Finn were supervising parking.

At the church end of the green, Nick was halfway through his archery demonstration.

Charlie had a loudspeaker and was giving a commentary. 'This is a recurve bow, which is light and easy to handle. Dad is going to show you what the correct stance is, how to hold the bow, how to grip the riser. He'll show you release techniques. Anyone know the name of the circular target that Dad is going to shoot at?'

'It's a roundel,' said a beaming parent.

'Another sign-up for the kids' archery club,' Zoe joked.

Over by the duck pond, excited children were queuing to throw wet sponges at Pete and Bob in the wooden stocks.

The chicks that Ellie had scared away with her scream a couple of nights earlier were back.

The most popular attraction was always the lambs and this year was no different. The farmer's wife was showing children how to feed the fluffy creatures and her husband was demonstrating sheepdog commands with their black-and-white Collie, Seth.

'What's going to happen with you and Dad?' Zoe asked.

'I don't know.'

'Because of Ruby?'

'No.' She faced Zoe. 'I'm stuck. Before Andrea, your dad was never unfaithful to me. I understand why he was. The thing is, it hurt so much, it nearly broke me, and I can't lay myself open to that again.'

'But you love each other, Mum.'

She nodded. 'I know.'

Chapter 43

4pm

It was mid-afternoon and Lower Wootton's village hall was packed. Charlie Matthews had rigged up a makeshift sound system. Garlands of bluebells lay with cream balloons on the trestle tables from the windmill open day.

It was as though everyone had been so thrown by the events of the past few days that they were even more determined to come out and celebrate Adrian and Jane's wedding which, only days earlier, had been tragically cut short by the discovery of Robert's body.

Ellie, Zoe, Finn, Sylvia, Simon and Jen sat at the same table.

Ellie watched as her family chatted and enjoyed the simple buffet which friends in the village had organised in place of the bride and groom's aborted catering.

All around them, neighbours were still reeling from the tragic deaths of Robert and Chrissy Seale. Relieved that their murderer was now in police custody, while also feeling sad about his age and circumstances, everyone seemed to be taking comfort in company and rituals. In music and food and dancing.

It had been a rollercoaster few days and Ellie felt dazed. Her world had been turned upside down and shaken. In addition to Robert and Chrissy's deaths, Ellie's life had been threatened, her business had been jeopardised, and she'd been sent nasty messages. She was pleased that the person who had sent her a death threat was no longer at large but was sad that it meant Liam would be facing very serious charges.

Ellie and Tracy had arranged a meeting with the man who had bought the cleaning franchise from Robert, and Dave was going to accompany them. They'd had a brief discussion via Zoom and Tracy had explained Robert's history. Ellie had mentioned 'business impersonation' and was hoping the man would accept his money back from Tracy, thereby releasing all his customers from their contracts. Meanwhile, she was busy devising ways to modernise Blix Blitz and to reward customer loyalty. Whereas she had been dreading doing this, and had put it off for years, she was already brimming with ideas for a pick-and-mix range of services which her cleaning customers could select, including window cleaning, car washing and laundry.

The bride and groom were on the floor, enjoying their first dance. Happiness radiated from Jane and Adrian's faces.

Movement in one corner of the hall caught Ellie's attention.

Dave nodded his apologies at the couple and made his way along the edge of the hall to his family's table. 'Unfortunately, I've been called into work, but I've come to join you for a few minutes, if that's OK.' He looked at Ellie and everyone else looked at her too.

Her heart gave a tiny leap. 'Sure,' she said, and everyone relaxed.

'Do you want a drink, Dad?' Zoe asked him. She pointed at a trestle table to the left of the stage where bottles and glasses nestled.

'I'll get a water. Anyone else want anything?'

'White wine for me, please,' said Sylvia, who already sounded a bit tipsy.

'When you come back, Simon and Jen want to show us something,' Ellie said to him.

It felt odd that only four days ago she and Dave had gone to Adrian and Jane's wedding together. They'd been to the bluebell woods on their first date in eighteen months. Their excitement had been tangible. And now, hope lay like a pricked balloon on the floor of Ellie's life.

Was Ruby going to leave Ellie alone?

She hoped so – but as for Dave, Ellie had no idea. And she knew that she couldn't do anything about it, just as she couldn't do anything about her own feelings.

Ruby had made things worse between her and Dave, but she hadn't created something that wasn't already there. It *was* more complicated for her than for Dave.

And that wasn't his fault or hers.

Perhaps she would never be able to trust him enough again to take the risk of being with him.

Inevitably, there would be another Andrea or Ruby, women who, like Ellie herself, loved Dave.

For now, though, Ellie wanted to concentrate on her family. Sylvia wanted to move to Lower Wootton permanently. Simon and Jen were going to get married, and she sensed there were changes ahead for Zoe and Finn.

Dave arrived back at the table with his bottle of water and a glass of wine for his mother.

Ellie felt his sadness.

In a way, it mirrored her own, but it was subtly different.

He would get back together with Ellie in a heartbeat, it seemed. But Ellie didn't know if she would ever be ready for this, or even if it was what she wanted anymore.

Sylvia took her glass of wine. 'Come on then, you two,' she said to her grandson and his fiancée. 'Show us.'

Simon took a small box out of his pocket. He flicked it open and eased a diamond engagement ring out of its hold. He pushed the beautiful ring on Jen's left hand, and they all cheered.

The music changed and ABBA began to play.

Sylvia squealed.

'Would you like to dance?' Simon asked his fiancée.

Jen giggled and got to her feet.

Ellie caught Dave looking at her and held his gaze for a few moments. She saw the longing in his eyes, the pain and regret, and for a few brief moments she wanted to melt into his arms and float round the dance floor with him. To forget everything that had happened. Forget Andrea and Ruby, and go back to being a a couple.

Then she remembered how she felt when she imagined him with Andrea. How she had felt when she thought something was going on with Ruby. And she knew: while she *couldn't* say never, she *couldn't* say now.

'Will you dance with your mum?' Sylvia asked Dave, oblivious of the moment that had just passed between him and Ellie. 'Your dad loved ABBA.' She stood up hopefully, swaying slightly.

Dave concealed a wistful sigh, then gave his mother a warm smile and held out his hand.

Ellie watched Simon and Jen and Sylvia and Dave head off to the dance floor.

Zoe and Finn shifted into the seats either side of Ellie.

'You alright?' Zoe asked her mum.

'As long as I have my family and friends.' She mustered a smile.

'Come and dance.' Finn held out his hand to Ellie.

'Thank you.' Ellie took a swig of wine and followed her daughter's boyfriend onto the dance floor.

Perhaps she would never be able to trust Dave enough again to take the risk of being with him.

But for now – this was more than enough. Wasn't it?

THE END

If you enjoyed Ellie, Zoe and Sylvia's story in this book, follow their adventures in the next one, *Murder in the Sunflower Field*, which is available on Amazon here. The blurb is this:

A DEAD CIRCUS PERFORMER.

THREE WOMEN SLEUTHS.

A NEW OWNER FOR THE WINDMILL?

It's summer in Lower Wootton and Ellie Blix is enjoying balmy evenings and barbecues. But family changes are afoot and she's unsettled. To make matters worse, a property developer has his sights set on the Blix family's windmill.

Then, a woman is found bludgeoned to death in a sunflower field, a Tarot card in her hand.

At first, Ellie's detective inspector ex-husband thinks the dead woman is Ellie. But she's soon identified as Tara Gables, a trapeze artist, who Ellie briefly met while walking the dog.

Tara's distraught partner is convinced that Ellie was the last person to see Tara alive. He pleads with the three Blix women to find out why his wife was walking in the fields when she was meant to be working.

When Ellie remembers Tara asking about a village tragedy from long ago, the three sleuths uncover a dark secret. If Ellie's suspicion is true, that the wrong person has been killed, they must identify the real target before there's another murder.

Order *Murder in the Sunflower Field* here.

About Author

Izzie Harper is the pen name of writer, teacher & story coach, Vicky Newham. Vicky lives on the south coast of England.

As Izzie Harper, she writes *The Wootton Windmill Mysteries*. The first of these, *Murder at the Christmas Carols*, was published on 21st November 2022, and *Murder in the Bluebell Woods* is the second.

Vicky's first crime fiction series was published by HQ/Harper Collins. Her debut in this police procedural series, *Turn a Blind Eye*, was optioned for TV and was shortlisted for the CWA John Creasey Debut Dagger in 2019. She has MAs in Creative Writing and Effective Learning.

Vicky divides her time between writing and teaching. She is passionate about helping other writers to craft their stories, and to make informed decisions about their publishing paths.

To keep up to date with Vicky's releases, special offers and promotions, please join her newsletter here.

If you like pictures of dogs, the sea, the Kent countryside and behind-the-scenes of Vicky's writing, you can follow her on Twitter at @VickyNewham and on Instagram at @vickynewhamwriter.

If you have enjoyed this story, Vicky would be hugely grateful if you could leave a quick review on Amazon and if you could tell your family and friends about it. Reviews and word-of-mouth recommendations are the *best* way to help authors.

And, if you haven't already, do order book 3 here. This is *Murder in the Sunflower Field,* and will publish in late summer – please check Amazon for exact publication dates.

Acknowledgments

When I was growing up, I adored reading Enid Blyton. The books were such fun and I longed to climb through the pages and join the characters on their adventures. I quickly moved onto Agatha Christie. When I was studying for my French A-level, I read Georges Simenon. With Christie and Simenon, it wasn't about the adventure. It was about the puzzle and the detection. All three authors set off a lifelong love affair with mysteries. I have continued to read them prolifically – and adore writing them.

During the COVID pandemic and associated lockdowns, I found myself wanting to write stories which were lighter in tone than my previous gritty, urban police procedurals. I didn't want to write gory corpse scenes, or go into detail about murder methods and forensics. I wanted to write about a community where people cared about each other. I wanted to write stories which featured warmth, humour and friendship more prominently. And I wanted to write about characters who aren't constrained by police procedures. Characters who can get away with the things that detectives cannot.

This is where I got the idea for *the Wootton Windmill Mysteries*. I moved house during one of the UK lockdowns and across the fields from where I live in Kent is a 'smock' windmill. If you look on my social media, you'll see some photos of it. I kept thinking about what an amazing home it would be for my main character. Ripple Windmill isn't converted into a home. It's been lovingly restored by the owners to a working mill. No longer in use, except for open days. I have moved the mill, and many other local landmarks, to create my fictional village of Lower Wootton.

I hope you enjoy reading about these characters as much as I am enjoying writing about them.

Please note: I am a British writer and I write using British English. This story is set in an English village and the manuscript has been edited and proofread by British professionals. A few spellings, terms and words may, therefore, be different for some readers. I've tried to ensure, however, that the meaning is clear for everyone.

Writing a novel is a team effort. I come up with the plot and characters, and write the words, and other people contribute at various stages. Without their input and magic, this story would not have made it into print.

I owe massive thanks to the following people for their help. To each of you, please know that I appreciate you. You are, in no particular order: Lynne Francis, Roz Watkins, Louise Voss, Alexandra Benedict, Lucy Lawrie, Keith Skinner, Sandra Mangan, Emmie Ellis. Apologies to anyone I've temporarily forgotten.

Made in the USA
Middletown, DE
24 April 2023